Justith
your comments
helped me write this
book. Thanks so
very much.
Bill

THE VOTING DEAD PROJECT

Bill Smith
May 2023

BILL SMITH

a novel

For Lynn and Cynthia
Best Friends Forever

ACKNOWLEDGEMENTS

Thank you, Gary Scott, for helping me transition from academic to fiction writing. I'm indebted to the following people who read early drafts of *The Voting Dead Project*. Thanks to Jenn Bradley, Al Hirsch, and Steve James for their reader's comments. I deeply appreciate Catherine Shornick, Burl Harmon, and Judith Page of WWU's Retirement Association Writing Group 2 for their edits and revision suggestions. I'm indebted to Mark Sherman, Don Mitchell, and Kerry Mitchell, who advised me early in my writing and introduced me to some helpful books.

At the last minute, two amazing beta readers stepped in and offered their opinions on characters and narrative flow as well as a number of edit suggestions. Thank you, Sean Dalgarn and Judy Foley. And thanks to Ashley Lefeat, a writer and Bellingham's most adequate D&D Dragon Master, whose suggestions clarified a number of character flaws.

My deep gratitude goes to Dr. Aden Ross, a longtime friend, well-published writer, dramatist, and author of *The Round Prairie Wars* (2022), who recommended developmental edits and amazing character suggestions. Her gentle nudges clarified my vision.

Finally, once again heartfelt thanks to Lynn Graham, my dear best friend, spouse, and longtime editor for her incredibly insightful proofreading and astute line editing suggestions on numerous versions leading to the final draft.

Thank you all so very much! Without you all, *The Voting Dead Project* would still be lingering in my mind.

TABLE OF CONTENTS

CADEN'S QUEST
QUEST
(SEPTEMBER 18, 2020 TO OCTOBER 1, 2020)

CHAPTER 1:
WTF
(SEPTEMBER 18, 2020)

Caden Cole unfolds yesterday's Bellingham Herald lying on his favorite sidewalk table at Cafe Kaffeine's streatery. He sets his steaming soy mocha down and scans the paper. The front page describes mask protocols, store closures, and an update about the ongoing investigation of an unidentified headless and handless man found fourteen months ago.

"The shaken newlywed couple was taking photos and selfies during low tide at Drayton Harbor, WA. Focusing on his bikini-clad wife with White Rock, British Columbia, in the background, the husband stepped backwards, tripped on a rock, and fell onto a body covered in seaweed. His right elbow pushed into the torso's bloated stomach and a foul-smelling spray spewed through the open neck gap onto the back of his head. As her husband passed out, the young woman noticed a blood-stained University of Utah tee shirt on the body."

The story ends with the wife's comment, *"Sean's almost off his meds, and his therapist told me he's so much better now."* This scene flashes through Caden's mind as a great opening for a horror film!

Between sips, he wonders how he'd film the burst of body spray, maybe a yellow puff that contrasts with the water surrounding it. The wife could also puke a green puddle on the rock near the body. Caden nods and smiles.

He's got time to kill. Covid put his vampire research project on hold, so for two hours every morning, he explores streets near his apartment. When he finds empty tables six feet apart at a streatery, he orders a mocha, grabs a local newspaper, and reads daily news before jotting down research notes in his iPad.

The image of the U of U tee shirt flits across his mind. For some reason, his best friend Ben Dunn wore his U of U tee shirt to class every Friday, even on snowy days. He smiles, remembering Ben's self-posted obituary in their office, "Ben Dunn died as expected."

A few younger people with rain dripping off their jackets, probably college students, sit at the table nearest him. No one carries an umbrella. Two of them have sunglasses on. Sipping the last of his mocha, Caden stares at Cafe Kaffeine's masked barista on her way to clear off the two other tables. She stops and bends over to pick up a paper cup under the table across from him. He feels the cold wind and adjusts his neck gaiter. Looking at her warms him and makes him smile.

Caden goes inside to the counter, orders another mocha, and buys a copy of today's *Herald*. He passes the barista and notices "M.J." on her name tag. He plops down at his outside table and wonders who M.J. looks like without a mask.

She's his favorite barista with an uncanny memory and red streaked black hair always in a ponytail. He dreams of nibbling her neck. What he can see of her face reminds him of Dakota Fanning in *Please Stand By*, the last film he and Ben saw together. He unfolds today's *Herald*, scans Trump's daily blame games, squabbles, and new hilarious "witch hunt" conspiracy theories. He wishes Ben could chat with him about the past two years of U.S. politics. They need another good pot chat.

A few slurps into his mocha, a headline in the local section slaps him in the face, "Blaine Murder Victim Identified":

"Dr. Benjamin Nathan Dunn, a reclusive but well-known Seattle tech consultant, was identified by the Whatcom County Coroner's Office after a DNA match from the FBI. Dunn's body was found in Drayton Harbor, Blaine, WA, on July 20, 2019. Police are asking anyone with information about Dunn to contact them."

For the next half hour, he sits still, stares at the paper, and shakes his head. Passing by, M.J. puts her hand on his shoulder and asks, "Are you O.K?"

He nods, "Yeah."

A few minutes later, he enters Cafe Kaffeine, puts his paper cup in the recycle bin, kicks the trash can inside the door, and knocks over the cart holding used coffee mugs and wine glasses. The noise draws attention to him standing among shards of broken glass and pieces of ceramic cups.

That evening, tipsy from a few Boundary Bay Brewery ales, he stumbles past the children's playground by the renovated Granary and stops near the lighted three-story tall Acid Ball at Waypoint Park. He picks up fist-sized beach rocks at the water's edge, and throws them at two barges moored across the narrow waterway.

All night, he dreams of Ben and their gorging on vegan donuts near Temple Square and semi-drunken walks in City Creek Canyon and in the foothills near the "U" on the hill above the University. He never laughed as much as he did with Ben. He twists and murmurs over and over, "Not Ben…not Ben."

CHAPTER 2:
THE CODED LETTER
(SEPTEMBER 21, 2020)

On Monday morning, Caden tears up junk mail at the post office a few blocks west of his apartment. He notices "B4L" on the return address on the last envelope. He opens it and sees this message dated June 18, 2019, two days before Ben's body was found:

2 % ^ *13 ^19 20 @ 18 ^* *2 $ 24* *! 20* *!14 20 # 17 % @* *13 ! 12 12*

On the flip side of the page was

11 # 19 19 *13 ^* *2 % 20 20* *^ $ 2* *2 4 12*

Ben developed his famous therapy code in grad school to keep their comments about faculty and other TAs secret. His office mates wrote their gripes on two large white boards, and no one outside their office group could interpret them. Walking home, Caden remembered Ben's simple code:

- Number letters of the alphabet from 1 to 26;

- Replace vowels (A,E,I,O,U, and Y) with the symbols above numbers 1-6 on your keyboard: A = !, E= @, I = #, O = $, U = %, and Y = ^

- Italicize numbers to keep them as numbers: *3 4 % 4 @ 19* = "3 dudes" (i.e. *3* = 3; 4 = D; % = U; 4 = D; @ = E; 19 = S)

- Begin and end words with* (For example, "Idiot" is *# 4 # $ 20*.

"Buy mystery box at antique mall. Kiss my butt."

Ben ended with his signature closing: *^ $ 2*, YOB, "Your Orphan Brother."

Caden shakes his head, "Jesus, why this letter now more than a year after your murder? When did you mail it? How did you know I was in Bellingham? Are you really dead?"

After dinner, he searches "Benjamin Nathan Dunn" to make sure he's dead, not just pranking him again like he did three times during grad school when he received calls from *Salt Lake Tribune* "reporters." Each one wanted to interview him about Ben, whose body had been found over the years in Mill Creek Canyon, Parley's Canyon, and Emigration Canyon—all hiking accidents.

As expected, Ben pops up as a tech writing consultant, usability guru, and CEO of Enraptured Users, well-known from Silicon Valley to Seattle. He vanished from public view early last year. With the exception of the *Herald*'s obituary, he can't find on People Search or WhitePages.com any more info about his death.

Walking to his apartment, he replays their past. In 2013 during their second year in the U's doctoral program, Caden's parents died on New Year's Day in an accident on a rain slick overpass in Jacksonville, N.C., his home town. After he returned to Salt Lake City from their funeral, Ben slipped a handwritten note into his English department mail box, and for the first time acknowledged him, "We're both orphans. My parents died during Thanksgiving vacation in an avalanche on their Colorado ski trip. Let's grieve together. 'YOB,' Your Orphan Brother, Ben."

Until graduation in 2016, they rambled through downtown Salt Lake City and City Creek Canyon. Ben's parents had practically disowned him when he turned down admission to Yale to join the Marine Corps. His father, founder and CEO of a large New York investment firm, viewed Ben's enlistment as giving him the finger. At the will reading he learned his father almost removed him from their estate which included three East Coast vacation homes, an Oregon beach house, and several million dollars' worth of stock shares. "Almost" because his mother wrote in an estate letter, "Enough of vengeance. Ben will get the Oregon beach house and four million dollars on his 50th birthday." His estranged older sister received the rest of the estate.

He told Caden, "When the rising sun sifts through the clouds over the Wasatch range, I imagine my dad's face glowering at me, and then I go for a few beers."

Caden's past didn't capture Ben's interest because his parents were working class high school graduates. Once over their second growler, Caden told him, "Our vacations always took place twelve miles away at a beach on Topsail Island a couple of Saturday nights a year. We fished and slept on folding lawn chairs under fishing piers. Depending on the season, we always went home with a cooler filled with spots, croakers, mullets, bluefish, and sometimes, a flounder."

After paying off his parents' funeral, medical expenses, and selling their home, Caden said, "I now have $12,000, an amazing gift from Mom and Dad!" When he told his story, Ben squinted and stared at the horizon.

Some weekends, they ambled through Salt Lake City, mostly to food trucks at City Creek Center and from Trolley Square to Liberty Park. Once they explored Saltair, a few miles from SLC, so Caden could visit the setting in *Carnival of Souls,* one of his favorite 60's horror films. There's something about seeing salt water and snow-capped mountains at the same time.

After a few months, Caden felt Ben was the big brother he always wanted, and his only friend since high school. He called them "BFL, Brothers for Life," and Ben smiled, nodding in agreement.

Ben provided for himself like the rest of them, but his VA education benefits and his paid teaching fellowship kept him financially better off than most in their cohort. In summers most English TAs waited on tables or worked in department stores. Ben edited documents and wrote user manuals for local high-tech start-ups. In the evenings he took his bosses' out-of-town clients to dinner and afterwards to jazz concerts, musicals, and plays at local theaters. "Damn, I get free meals and $200 per client event on top of my weekly earnings."

Ben made more in ten days than the rest of them did in the ten-week summer. They missed him when he moved to Seattle to make more money than they ever would in education. But mostly they missed the monthly dinner parties he treated all of them to at local expensive restaurants, places they only dreamed about. Servers, especially older women, cooed "the Doll" as soon as he walked in the front door. Some, impressed with his height and dark eyes, even said, "Look, it's Lucifer Morningstar!"

At graduation, Ben waved his PhD diploma in front of his face like a paper fan on a hot day. Then he turned his back on academia. The last time the cohort saw him, he seemed sad for them, and shook his head, frowning as he left them sitting in the food truck court at City Center.

They became distant friends after graduation. Ben created Enraptured Users, LLC, and moved to Seattle. Caden accepted a tenure-track teaching position at Virginia Commonwealth University, in Richmond, Virginia, where he taught film studies, mostly horror and disability films.

During the 2017 Christmas holidays, a year after his move, Ben sent Caden a 1st class round-trip Delta ticket to Seattle, an unexpected Christmas gift. Rather than staying in his upscale condo outside Seattle, Ben booked one of the best scenic hotels overlooking Elliott Bay within walking distance of everything he thought Caden would enjoy, including an Underground Paranormal Experience tour, the Seattle Art Museum, and the Gold Rush Museum. From the picture windows of their high-rise suite, they watched ferries, Alaska cruise ships, Foss Super Tugs, and container ships inch across the sound filled with white caps and thick dark curling clouds lurking above them.

Their first night, Caden showed Ben real estate brochures of condos and townhouses along the James River, south of Richmond. Smiling, he said, "Visiting me will be your first upscale Southern couch surfing excursion."

They chilled and spent three days riding ferries, drinking local microbrews, eating dark chocolate, gorging on vegan food near Capitol Hill, exploring haunted buildings, and smoking too much recreational weed from pot stores near Fisherman's Wharf. Caden remembered standing for hours in the MoPOP, staring at Jimi Hendrix memorabilia.

Outside a chocolate store in Pike Place Market, Ben asked, "How the hell did you get so interested in horror films?"

"On Saturday nights in bad weather, Dad and I watched horror films while Mom sat at the kitchen table and worked on jigsaw and crossword puzzles. She said, 'I don't invite horror into my home,' so we gave her a headset so she could ignore us. We must have seen sixty movies while I was in high school."

Caden told Ben tales about his film studies classes, especially parodies by horror film students. "In one group's *The Last Movie* when a monster stepped from the movie screen and sliced off the head of a first-row viewer, three dating couples ran upstairs to the projection room rather than out the theater doors. The monster followed them into the room without an exit, an homage to *The Blob*. They nailed that stereotype of naive young people."

The next morning in SeaTac, Ben stopped at a small vegan dessert stand, "We need two Nanaimo bars for me and my Southern orphan brother." From that moment on Ben vacillated between calling him an SOB and YOB.

One bite, and Caden was hooked. He chomped down his bar as the gate staff announced, "First Class passengers, please present your boarding passes!"

At the check-in stand, Ben handed him an autographed first edition copy of Stephenie Meyers' *Twilight*, the first book in her vampire series.

"Check out Forks, WA…it might scratch your horror film itch. Next summer we'll explore the Olympic Peninsula and check out local brews and vampire news."

Caden winced at the internal rhyme, as Ben backed away smiling. By the time he entered the plane, the Nanaimo bar and his Seattle visit were unforgettable pleasant memories.

In late spring 2018, Ben visited him at VCU. As a consultant for VCU's Registrar and Admissions offices, Ben helped plan their next two-year budget cycle by capturing trends in registration data, i.e., student dropout rates, family income, gender, race, age, the length of time they stayed in college until they dropped out, why they dropped out, and when they returned, if they did.

One mid-West college he consulted for based its 1st year offerings on the dropout rate, but didn't realize over half of those dropouts returned within five years to finish their degrees. Their long-term enrollment was constantly growing, not receding. Ben's takeaway was, "Dropouts should be cultivated, not ignored." He breathed data. Big orgs. loved him; that's why he moved to Seattle.

Caden last heard from Ben in January 2019. In his predictably late New Year's letter, Ben wrote, "My dear SOB, just signed 'a jaw-dropping contract' with an anonymous shadow company! Going dark to design user-testing protocols. I'll keep in touch."

Attached to the note was a cashier's check for $40,000, a down payment on Caden's townhouse. Ben's note at the bottom of the page, "To make sure my first Southern couch surfing experience is memorable—B4L, YOB," made Caden's jaw drop.

CHAPTER 3:
THE ANTIQUE MALL
(SEPTEMBER 22, 2020)

C aden learns "Penny Lane Antique Mall," a Bellingham Antique store, is four blocks west of his apartment, only a block from the Granary at Waypoint Park, where he sometimes drinks kombucha and watches young women enter and exit the yoga studio. Walking in the drizzle past the county museum, he notices the words in a large red and white circle painted on the side of an old brick building, "Bellingham: The City of Subdued Excitement." He takes a photo to share with his VCU students, then a selfie. He captions the photo, "A good motto for nearly every city in the world during the Pandemic."

He walks down the concrete steps, crosses Marine Heritage Park to Penny Lane, and stands outside the store, reading mask rules taped to the large street windows. Reflected behind him in the glass is Whatcom Museum with dark ominous clouds moving over it. Caden smiles and wonders if Ben's dad is frowning down on him.

The only customer, he stares across the large shop past the clear plastic screen protecting the cashier. He notices a handwritten "Mystery Box" note pointing to a small wooden box shaped like a tiny coffin sitting on an antique oak bookcase. Since Ben sent him a coded anonymous letter, he's cautious and careful. He spies a pair of geode book ends on a table near the window and buys them first to cover his tracks.

On the way to pick up the geodes, he passes Ben's sealed $50 mystery box, and asks, "What's in the mystery box?"

The masked old hippy at the cash register stares at him for at least 30 seconds, shakes his head, "I don't know…it's a mystery, dude."

Caden picks up the dusty wooden box the size of a Christmas chocolate cordial box but weighing only a few ounces. He shakes it, and hears something sliding inside it.

"Can I get the geodes and the mystery box for $90?"

The geezer squints across the street at the Soy House and nods, "Yeah, brother."

CHAPTER 4:
BEN'S LETTER
(SEPTEMBER 23, 2020)

I n fall semester 2019, Caden applied for a sabbatical. His film studies dissertation, *The Economic Impact of Horror Films,* and his fascination with the *Twilight* series, introduced last year by Ben, convinced him to submit his sabbatical research project: "Forks' Vampire Economy and the Future of Horror Films."

He told his classes, "Vampire films are waning, and zombie movies are rising in the West Coast with *iZombie* in Seattle and *Santa Clarita Diet* in California. Even the Irish zombie musical *Anna and the Apocalypse* suggests rising international zombie interest. And *Dead End Drive,* a short zombie apocalypse film with a cast of riveting actors, some with disabilities, appeared this year at the Lennard Davis Disability Film Festival in San Francisco. When you consider the impact of climate change and world politics, you can see why zombies are rising from their graves to enter the world they once knew. Just like in the graveyard in *Night of the Living Dead,* we can hear a man's warning echoing across the U.S. 'They're coming to get you, Barbara.'"

Before Halloween, at least one third of his students played zombie games on campus, zigzagging from classroom to classroom with arms outstretched, groaning loudly. Few of them knew of the Richmond vampire, the Hollywood Cemetery urban legend based on the Church Hill Tunnel collapse in 1925. None of them knew of A. A. Carr's *Eye Killers*, a novel which blends together European vampire and Navajo legends.

But they all knew Buffy, Angel, the *Twilight Series*, Ann Rice's *The Vampire Chronicles*, *The Vampire Diaries*, and even *The Lost Boys*. More students than he imagined knew Christopher Moore's vampire trilogy, *Blood Sucking Fiends*. The series *Post Mortem: No One Dies in Skarnes* convinced him the concept of vampirism was changing and becoming popular again. Vivian Shaw's novels might be leading the pack.

Once he told Ben, "Vampire women are sexier than zombie women. I see no joy in watching a wide-eyed, rotting faced woman moan at me with someone's bloody ear hanging out her mouth." Ben responded, "An ear's a hell of lot better than a testicle."

He enjoyed watching vampire films, especially romantic gothic ones. The zombie exception is watching gorgeous white-haired zombie Liv Moore in *iZombie* mix human brains with fresh fruit and smile as she eats them. "Something about her eyes turns me on. But when it gets down to it, I'd rather be a zombie than a vampire in a film because I like the way they move."

Earlier during Spring break, he visited Forks on the Olympic Peninsula and met with members of the Chamber of Commerce and small business owners. In the first six years after Amazon's 2005 release of the *Twilight Vampire Saga* series, more than 70,000 Twi-fan tourists visited Forks with its population of nearly 3,800 and the surrounding areas, to explore Bella Swan's homeplace. Fans took selfies where vampire Edward Cullen hung out. Caden's sabbatical proposal contained letters of support from Forks' business owners on the importance of his research project. VCU awarded him a one-year sabbatical beginning Fall 2020.

In a *VCU News* "Faculty Interview" section Caden said, *"Zombie apocalypse films depict end-of-the-world scenarios. At first glance it's hard to tell the differences between fictional crumbling infrastructures, devastated towns and cities, and the current rising rates of poverty and homelessness mirrored in these films caused by self-centered politicians, partisan politics, scared citizens, and greedy corporations, not zombies."*

Focusing on his sabbatical research project, he told the reporter, *"Who wants to visit the creepy locations of decaying urban landscapes people are fleeing in the Walking Dead rather than the beautiful pristine landscape of the Olympic Peninsula, where young vampires often act romantically with their current and future peers? Even so, I've added to my cell contacts the phone number of the 'Walking Dead' tours in Senoia, Georgia, my back-up, in case I have to shift focus from vampires to zombies because of the political climate."* He imagined Ben saying, "That sucks," unaware of the pun.

Caden arrived at SeaTac, realizing his trip to Forks was now just for research. He and Ben planned to attend the virtual Forever Twilight in Forks Festival in mid-September and explore local Peninsula film sites, but Covid and Ben's disappearance and murder gutted his dream.

In early August, Caden relocated to Bellingham for six months during his sabbatical to research *Twilight's* impact on local income. B'ham was cheaper to live in than Seattle, but more expensive than Richmond.

On his blog, he told his students, "Almost everything I need is within five blocks of my apartment, including six pot shops, nearly a dozen breweries, and several plant-based food trucks and restaurants. I lost track of coffee shops because you can get an incredible cup of fresh local brew almost anywhere. Of course, I'm writing this note at Cafe Kaffeine's streatery.

"The bus station is across the street from my apartment and in less than ten minutes I can get to Squalicum Harbor Marina, historical

Fairhaven district (a tourist mecca), Western Washington University's library, and the Pacific Northwest Archives building, an archival center containing info on tourism and the Washington economy. The city library is only three blocks from my apartment. I seldom need to rent a car. The only drawback is I can't get sweet iced tea any place. Go figure."

Before moving to B'ham, a VCU student and Navy vet suggested he read all three of Bellingham writer Clyde Ford's Charlie Noble mysteries. A retired Coast Guard Commander, Noble lived on his boat moored in Squalicum Harbor, a mile from Caden's apartment. From Ford, he learned the types of boats moored in the Marina, the names of the visible islands in the sound, and restaurants Noble frequented, especially Old Town Cafe, famous for its vegan meals. More than a decade had passed since Ford's books had been published, so some places mentioned in them had closed, but the ones still open were worth the walk.

Even better, as Ben would have pointed out, "Bellingham with a population slightly larger than 90,000 is the closest contiguous U.S. city to Canada, less than a 30-minute drive to the border." For Ben, it would have been Bellingham's border location that captured him. He used to tell their graduate clan, "I want my ashes spread in Canada!"

Caden liked the fact that from his apartment he can drive from sea level to Artist Point at 5,100 feet above Bellingham Bay and stare at Mount Baker, rising another 5,500 feet, just an hour from B'ham. He felt a Saltair vibe when he walked around the marina and stared at snow-capped mountains.

Covid changed everything. After he arrived, the ferry schedule to the Peninsula went on hold, so he can't visit Forks and surrounding areas and take photos of places mentioned in the *Twilight* series. Now he spends most of his time taking virtual notes on the Olympic Peninsula which he could have done much cheaper in Richmond. He daily searches ProQuest and EBSCO and Zooms owners of struggling tourist Olympic Peninsula businesses, mostly cafes and curio shops.

After dinner, he removes the thin wax seal from the mystery coffin. A carved Confederate flag decorates the underside of the lid. Inside is a match box covered in bubble wrap fastened with two rubber bands, and a folded envelope with "The VD Project" hand-printed on it.

"VD my butt! I swigger…did I just blow $50 on another one of Ben's jokes?" He opens the match box and finds a small thumb drive.

The envelope contains a short letter from "Dr." Benjamin Dunn. Caden couldn't remember the last time Ben called himself "Doctor."

"*July 18, 2019*

I'm Dr. Benjamin Nathan Dunn, research specialist and lead consultant on "The Verifying Data Project." As a tech writing consultant and usability designer, I massage product data, observe actual users, and write protocols so everyone can easily and safely use the product.

In early 2019, I moved to Washington primarily because of high tech start-ups, but coffee shops, cool weather, views of the bay, mountains, and quick access to Canada sealed the deal. I went dark. A group I call "the Council of 5" asked me to supervise their Verifying Data Project, a study of data from two Southern cemeteries. The salary offer was unbelievable, so I put Enraptured Users, my private consulting business, on hold. As their project director, I embraced the VD Project, which was beginning in N.C. and VA, and eventually moving across the South to cemeteries in other states.

The enclosed thumb drive has my journal of the VD Project's findings, and our project's potential impact on future Presidential elections as early as 2024. As I analyzed data, I should have seen where the research was taking us, and why it was happening now, and for that I'm sorry. I'm going darker, moving to Canada, hoping to live like the elderly hermits in And the Birds Rained Down. *I apologize for my role in the VDP's burgeoning success.*

I hope whoever finds this jump drive will let the public know how easily social media can manipulate us with false information and stack the cards in favor of theatrical unthinking politicians, and the invisible unknown wealthy. If the VD Project succeeds, America will return to its pathetic past and benefit the rich in unimaginable ways—all based on our new nefarious model of voter suppression.

Regrettably,

Benjamin Nathan Dunn, PhD.

Owner, Enraptured Users, LLC"

Staring out his window at nearly empty buses, Caden is relieved "VD" means "Verifying Data,' and wonders about the "Verifying Data Project." What data do we need to verify and what is "a new nefarious model of voter suppression?" All night long questions fly through his mind like sparrows through a mead hall.

His weekend drags by because fewer business owners in Forks and surrounding peninsula communities contact him to Skype or Zoom about the economic impact of the *Twilight* days. Two restaurant owners told him about their pandemic business losses and future fears. Last week one motel owner complained, "The recent Antifa bus scandal two weeks after George Floyd's death didn't help boost tourism either."

Caden has fewer than 100 days to solve Ben's murder. He'll continue his vampire research about the Peninsula until his apartment contract ends in early January 2021, and he heads back to Richmond during Spring break. He's uneasy about Ben's job and needs help finding his killers. He wonders how he received Ben's letter in Bellingham, more than a year after his murder. He needs a local researcher to find links to Ben's murder while he focuses half his time on his sabbatical project.

CHAPTER 5:
CADEN'S SEARCH BEGINS
(OCTOBER 1, 2020)

O ver his steaming morning mocha, Caden watches three young women move from store to store, taping "Black Lives Matter" posters on storefront windows. Five older men dressed in REI's finest sit at two small square tables under the plastic canopy above Cafe Kaffeine's outside tables. They lean into one another, laughing at the young women with their "Black Lives Matter" signs. One of them shouts, "All Lives Matter," and they toast by bumping their coffee mugs. M.J. stares at them. One nervously twists his wedding ring and opens and closes his fist.

M.J. pauses, stands with a rag and a clear blue spray bottle, rolls her eyes, glances quickly at Caden, and from two tables away explains loudly and calmly through her mask, "'Black Lives Matter' raises our awareness of the pain systemic racism creates and perpetuates. For centuries, 'Black,' not 'white' lives, haven't really mattered. 'Black Lives Matter' exposes centuries of America systematically ignoring and mistreating Black people. Trayvon Martin, George Floyd, Breonna Taylor, Elijah McClain, and thousands of others put faces and stories on the hidden truths 'Black Lives Matters' reveals. We don't need to say 'White Lives Matter' or 'All Lives Matter' because we act as if they always have."

She bends over, picks up a napkin, captures Caden's gaze and his thoughts, and sprays the next table. The men sit in silence and look away from one another. She glares at them and for the first time Caden notices her delicate antique gold wedding ring, a piece of jewelry that sends his romantic hopes swirling down the drain like a kid's favorite marble in an elementary school toilet.

All of the men look down silently. A few minutes later, one geezer stands, shakes his head, "Thank you. We understand now. Please accept our apology for laughing." She nods at him, finishes her table, and goes inside. They stare after her and talk quietly. As they leave, each one places a $20 tip under his coffee cup.

Caden peeks over his *Herald*, watches M.J. clear their tables, and pocket the tips in her tight slacks. He tells his iPhone, "Learn more about M.J." Her confidence and outspokenness remind him of Aslyn Williams, his former teaching assistant and current adjunct faculty member who corrects him and teaches him something about racism in almost every class.

One evening, Aslyn told his horror film class, "A spoiler alert: don't get too attached to the Black characters, they usually get killed first, unless you're Ben in *Night of the Living Dead*, then you're last, shot by white folks because you're mistaken for a zombie. Yeah…right." She held her hands up and curved her fingers in air quotes when she said "mistaken." Later she introduced Jordan Peele's *YouTube* interviews to his horror film class and won him over.

Aslyn is now teaching his 200-level intro to horror film class. During his sabbatical year, she and her husband, Tyrone Jones, both former Marines, are living in his new townhouse at James River's Edge Estates outside Richmond. An economic win-win for all of them.

At his apartment Caden plugs in Ben's jump drive and skims his journal entries, twenty-two of them from December 29, 2018 to

July 18, 2019. The only recurring people in the early entries are Dr. August Humphrey and Dr. Jackson Canaday, whose name sounds familiar. With decreasing vampire tourism news, Caden has more time to make Ben's murder his top priority.

Dr. Humphrey's easy to find online. At 60, he's a well-known respected scholar who holds an endowed History Professorship and serves as Chair of the Division of U.S. History, Political Science, and Cultural Studies at Wilmington City College, a small posh private school in Wilmington, North Carolina. He's on leave completing a Southern history research project; info confirmed later in Ben's journal. When Caden Googles "Dr. Jackson Canaday," his obituary and his photo pop up. Caden mumbles, "Crap on a crouton!"

He recognizes Jackson from high school, a tall good-looking popular long-distance runner, one of the few seniors who noticed him and smiled every time he saw him. At 36, he was an Assistant Professor of History and Political Science in his fourth year at Wilmington City College. He was an innovative teacher, adored by students, judging from the turnout at his memorial service. He drowned during a storm at Topsail Island, N.C. Flounder fishers found his body during low tide late at night on July 16, 2019, in a mudflat near North Topsail Bridge.

"I swanee…four days before Ben!" Caden stares out his window and counts bus passengers still in single digits. He returns to Ben's journal entries looking for danger signs and patterns.

Ben and Jackson are his top priorities. He needs more info about Humphrey and the VD Project. What did they do for the project and what was Jackson's relationship with Ben? Edgy, he walks over to Aslan Brewery, sits outside near a table heater, and orders a growler of Charley Foxtrot. Jerome, Aslyn's husband, once told him Charlie Foxtrot means clusterfuck in the military. Since Growing Veterans, a local "dirt therapy" non-profit, grows Aslan's organic hops, the brew's name makes sense during Covid. He raises his glass, "I'll nail the bastards. It's just a matter of time, my orphan brother…just a matter of time!"

All afternoon he drinks Charlie Foxtrot and reads about Drayton Harbor, where the couple found Ben's body. He wonders which side of the border Ben might have lived on. Ben's first journal entry begins on December 29, 2018, the day he signed his VDP contract. Caden thinks about the "Verifying Data" Project and voter suppression. Why did Ben continue with the VDP anyway?

Caden was never sure if Ben liked money or its lifestyle, something most TAs saw as the same thing. He remembers the time Ben caught the attention of one TA, a cowboy from the Intermountain West, who misheard their conversation during a group lunch at a local bar about Ben's focus on money. Slamming down his growler, he said, "He loves bucks! I didn't know he was a deer hunter! Damn, how'd I miss that?" From then on, when Ben wasn't around, they all called him BCB, "Buck Chaser Ben."

By the time he returns to Cafe Kaffeine, it's closed. He'd missed his chance to chat with M.J. At home, he slides Ben's drive into his computer and begins his first thorough reading of his journals, hoping to channel some of Ben's VD vibes.

BEN'S FIRST
THUMB DRIVE
ENTRIES
(DECEMBER 29, 2018 TO APRIL 16, 2019)
&
CADEN'S
COMMENTS

December 29, 2018: Contract at Squalicum Marina, Bellingham, WA

An anonymous dude texted me to meet him at Squalicum Harbor Marina in Bellingham, WA. I sat at the only wooden table outside the Web Locker Restaurant, as directed. The cold wind whipped across the bay and made my eyes water. At 1:15 a grey-bearded man carrying two steaming paper cups sat down across from me, handed me a sugar-free decaf, hemp mocha—my favorite—and introduced himself as a corporate lawyer. He gave me a large envelope with a job offer and told me to sign the enclosed contract by 2:30 today.

He stood up, grabbed his mocha, and said, "I'll give you time to think about our offer. I'll return before 2:30." He pulled his hood over his head, tightened it, and walked down the dock to look at boats near Gate 4. He tossed his mocha into the garbage can. I muttered, "What the hell, I could have drunk that mocha!"

The envelope held a job offer, a contract, and a privacy agreement, all requiring I become invisible. At the end of the contract was a jaw-dropping offer: after taxes—$3,000 daily, plus business expenses, starting at 2:30 today until midnight November 5, 2028. If the project succeeded, and I remained silent, I'd receive the same daily salary for life. Attached to the packet was a reservation receipt for tonight's stay and dinner at the Hotel Bellwether on the shore of the Marina.

I figured I'd make a little over $1 million annually…for life! Matched with my mother's bequest, I can easily retire at 50. I smiled, knowing I had only fourteen more years of kissing people's asses before I became a multi-millionaire!

The old guy returned at 2:25. I calmly signed the contract as he watched. Then he signed as a witness. He removed his glove, shook my hand, and told me to expect a series of UPS deliveries over the next few days. "You have one week to go dark, so plan carefully as you disappear."

He placed the papers in the envelope. A purring chauffeured golden gull-wing Mercedes pulled up to the curb. He got in, nodded at me, and they drove off.

At the Web Locker's takeout window I ordered a veggie burger, stared at fishing boats, drooled at a 32-foot Targa, "the 4 by 4 of the sea," and watched white-capped waves moving across gray Bellingham Bay. I saw several of the San Juan Islands barely visible between the water and the clouds. At the Bellwether Hotel I leaned on the deck railing and enjoyed the cold wind as the sun set at 4:30.

For the next two hours, I searched Zillow and Redfin for Canadian condos. At $3,000 per day, I can afford a condo with an outstanding view. Hell, I could probably afford two on my 50th birthday. I fell asleep wondering how much a 32-foot Targa cost.

March 24, 2019: 1st Meeting with the Council of 5 at Vineyard Haven, Martha's Vineyard, MA

At 7:30 p.m. I arrived at my lodging, a one-room cabin on a hill overlooking a small old graveyard and the harbor. Through the fog I saw flickering lights from boats docked off shore and Oak Bluffs across the inlet. I walked past the tombstones, down into Vineyard Haven, and sadly learned the Black Dog Tavern closed early on Sundays. I traipsed back to my cabin munching on airline peanuts and a small packet of graham crackers.

The next morning at 10:00 a.m. I met my bosses (I call the Council of 5) in a three-story mansion at the end of a gated gravel road north of Vineyard Haven. Five senior white men, about my father's age, dressed business casual, sat in silence around a large polished mahogany dining table with their first names on placards: Thomas, Robert, Francis, William, and Jonathan. As William twisted his wedding ring, Jonathan stood, "We have one hour to fill you in and go over your responsibilities as the primary research consultant of VDP, the 'Verifying Data' Project!" Everyone nodded and smiled.

Thomas handed me a large envelope like the one before each of them. On his command, we opened them at the same time. Mine contained a flight ticket to Wilmington, N.C., info on two cemeteries to visit, one in Wilmington and one in Richmond, VA., and the Council's 2-phase priority list:

Phase 1: Data Collecting (2019-2020)
- Meet research teams at Oakdale and Hollywood cemeteries
- Review and verify researchers' data/findings
- Develop a user protocol for future researchers and their interns
- Develop and test a recipient questionnaire
- Create a graphic template of collected data

Phase 2: Future Site Selection (2020-2021)
- Select 40-50 large Southern cemeteries for future research

I wondered, "Why the hell Southern cemeteries?" but just listened for the next hour and took notes. They smiled as Thomas concluded, "We'll reconvene here next month on April 24. Thank you, Dr. Dunn."

When he nodded, we rose, and walked outside past the swimming pool and tennis court, into a large field bordering the edge of a cliff overlooking the Atlantic. As we stood and talked, mostly about the stock market and Wall Street, a Sikorsky helicopter, like the one used by Queen Elizabeth's family, landed on a large helipad. Each Council member shook hands with me and boarded the chopper.

It was 11:30 a.m., so I had the rest of the day to explore the island. I drove to Oak Bluffs, grabbed lunch and stopped in Edgartown to walk along the beach. I pretended Caden had never made us stream *Jaws* four times. After eating, I wandered across the island to Chilmark and then looped to Tisbury and back to my cabin, so I could brag one day to Caden I had explored Martha's Vineyard. I shook my head, realizing I earned $3,000 today and really enjoyed this project. I saw my father's disapproving face in the clouds above the horizon and went for a beer...O.K....four.

After dinner at the Black Dog, I stared across the harbor and glanced over the project outline. We're collecting data from grave-yards. WTF!

Caden's Comments

$3,000 daily…a bit more than an English professor makes! I see why you went dark. Jesus.

Deaf students in my "Images of Disability" classes always enjoy reading about the Vineyard because of its signing history and its 19th century Deaf community. I envy Ben: Martha's Vineyard and cemeteries. My horror film vibe twitches. What kind of data will the VDP collect at cemeteries? And why? Ben's cabin even looks across a cemetery.

March 26, 2019: Dr. August Humphrey (Wilmington, N.C.)

There're no non-stop flights from Martha's Vineyard to Wilmington, N.C. …seven and a half effing hours to get here…a day shot.

Then I remembered I earned $3,000 plus expenses regardless of what I did each day. I rented a Porsche Cayenne and drove to the Graystone Inn, a B&B in the historic district, a few miles from the nearly hundred-acre Oakdale Cemetery.

The next morning in the inn courtyard shaded by tall live oaks, Dr. August Humphrey, a History Professor from private Wilmington City College, introduced himself and three volunteer history interns as VD Project researchers. The interns kept glancing at the breakfast bar, so I ordered breakfast for us all.

While the interns explored Graystone's famous buffet, Humphrey said, "Call me 'Doctor,' not 'Professor.'"

"Call me Ben," I smiled, surmising he's a PDh, perpetual dick head, as well as a PhD.

He updated me on the VDP as I finished a slice of pecan pie that tasted almost as good as our family chef's. Dr. Humphrey glanced at his interns filling their plates, "My interns are students from families of wealthy university donors. Their fathers thought each of them needed more community service on their resumés."

He gave a quick overview of the VD Project which began a few months before the 2016 election.

"Our sponsors knew U.S. voters didn't want change; they yearned for the comfort and safety of the past, things they could reliably count on." He pointed to his cap, said "MAGA," and paused.

I noticed his MAGA cap was white with black letters, pooling into blood red puddles at the bottom of each letter, and casting an eerie dark creepy shadow. Gray tombstones with dollar signs filled the background, reminding me of a Stephen King book cover. It never occurred to me until looking at Dr. Humphrey's cap two MAGAs co-existed, something MAGA Don must know about.

Humphrey continued, "For two years, our bosses watched the President and his team feed the fears and hopes of financially insecure and scared voters. They predicted emotions would trump logic and personality trump leadership. They labelled real news 'fake news' and created the 'blame game' to deflect unwanted attention away from themselves. Social media and the news organizations jumped on it! Our motto for the VD Project is 'Verify...Not vilify!'"

I nodded, thinking, "Makes sense to me."

"By mid-2018 our bosses knew the time was ripe for a plan to preserve the American Dream. Based on social media's role in fake news and conspiracy theories embraced by popular political leaders, they designed the Verifying Data Project. A few months later, they launched the VDP to secure a future based on the past, the real past U.S. citizens shout about in bars, meetings, and churches, not like some whining Black or Latinx socialists do when they dream of the future. VDP is the answer to most people's dreams, even if they can't yet voice them. We can't change the past, but we can use the past to change the future."

He leaned back in his chair, swirled a silver spoon in his steaming tea cup and smiled, "The answer to our future is the path to the real past!" As he raised his cup, the interns returned, each holding two plates of food.

I pretended to be interested, as if the past really fucking mattered. Hell, there were no computers, internet, or social media in those days.

Between bites, Dr. Humphrey's interns talked non-stop about historical Oakdale Cemetery. They calmed down when they told me, "Oakdale is a memorial and resting place for approximately 18,000 Confederate soldiers and famous people such as Reverend Billy Graham, 'North Carolina's Favorite Son.'

"In 1867 the cemetery corporation gifted space to the Ladies Memorial Association. A few years later they placed a large bronze statue of a Confederate soldier near the Confederate Mound, where more than 300 unknown Confederate soldiers lie."

Dr. Humphrey interrupted, "Don't worry about the unknown dead. Our bosses are only interested in the known dead: Confederate veterans and their dead male descendants."

Another intern continued, "We're gathering data on the location of the graves of roughly 150,000 dead white men, confederate vets and their sons, born and buried in N.C. between 1863 and 1964. Our MAGA brothers are doing the same thing in Virginia."

The Jim Crow era flashed across my mind. I couldn't help myself, "Why North Carolina and Virginia cemeteries and graveyards?"

The oldest intern butted in, "The highest Confederate Civil War death rates occurred in N.C. and Virginia. Around 22% of the Confederate dead rest in these two states. Of course, not all deaths were combat related, but they're buried in these states, and we count them because their deaths matter, if we can know who they are. No matter how they died—combat, wounds, or disease—they're still

Confederates. Fewer than 200 federal troops are buried here, and few, if any, alleged Black Confederate soldiers."

Looking around, he leaned toward me and whispered, "Only White Male Deaths Matter. We don't visit graveyards anyway, only cemeteries. Graveyards mostly belong to churches and families, so they're usually smaller and private, and often Black. Data gathered at their burial places isn't worth the time it takes to write it down."

More questions popped up, but I kept quiet. I recalled my sergeant's words, "Assholes…Shut your mouths…Listen and Learn!" I hadn't quite figured out the research time frame and thought, "Why focus only on Southern cemeteries, and why are we verifying the known dead whose data should already be in the cemetery public records?"

The interns gave me a thumb drive with their collected data. As we drove to Oakdale, I listened to them blather on. All afternoon, they talked non-stop—yada, yada—about the importance of their research for future generations while I thought about the 101-year timeline, the Jim Crow era.

Every time I asked Dr. Humphrey a question about the project's timeline, he refocused us on data collection. I must have looked startled, OK…pissed. He shook his head, "Like you, I believe the timeline is bogus: it's too short."

I sat up and leaned into his conversation. "In 1835, N.C. lawmakers overruled the 1776 voting privilege act and by a very close vote eliminated the free Black vote. Since 1835 was a pivotal year, I've asked the Council to roll back the time frame to before the Civil War to increase the numbers in our database. The men who died before the Civil War probably held beliefs similar to Confederate veterans' beliefs."

I nodded, thinking, "What the hell! He's expanding the Jim Crow era."

An intern answered his cell phone, smiled, and stood up, "Mr. Yancey needs our help. He's waiting for us in section K near the

Mound to conduct the first Oakdale MAGA interview." The crew put on their disturbing MAGA hats and left smiling.

"Cemetery interviews!" I thought.

When he was sure they'd gone, Dr. Humphrey told me, "Expanding the project to 1835 gives us 25 more years to research across the South and easily increases our project's database by more than 25,000 deaths. With my new timeline we can survey cemeteries existing before the war, even here in Oakdale, which began in 1852. Our new timeline will give us 17 more years of data here at Oakdale alone. And better yet, it'll increase our income because it'll take more time to research! The new timeline will be profitable to us!"

He smiled, raised his hand and rubbed his thumb, index, and middle finger together. "I joined the VD Project in mid-2018 and signed a four-year contract as supervisor and head researcher. I plan to retire in 2022, so this extra income will let me live my retirement dream."

He pulled out his Android and showed me a photo of his new Albemarle 41 Custom Carolina Edition boat, "And make sure I retire early and expand my luxurious intracoastal waterway tours for rich lady Confederate descendants." He smiled and toasted me yet again with his almost empty tea cup.

I smirked and thought, "Only four paid years…rich lady Confederate descendants, my ass!"

That evening I read a tourist brochure at the reception desk. I understood why the Council selected Wilmington. During the Reconstruction, Wilmington with its biracial government was the ideal example of the post-war country moving forward. But in 1898, depending on who you're reading, an "insurrection," "mob," or "race riot," led by white supremacists burned down the African American newspaper building and murdered as many as 300 African American residents to make the Lost Cause rise again.

Of the 120,000 African American voters from a few years before the race riot, only 6,000 could still vote by 1904. The 1898 race riot was the only insurrection in U.S. history to overthrow a local government. In less than a decade the Old South rose again, and Wilmington's politics, like Richmond's, shouted, "Jim Crow and the Lost Cause."

Caden's Comments

I realize Ben earned his nickname, "BCB." At least he's still buying lunch for his interns. The last things I thought about before my nightly Shudder binge were, "What new data are they gathering, and why don't they just use cemetery records? Who is Yancey Jenkins, and why, and how's he conducting interviews with dead people?"

Just thinking about Wilmington reminds me of the race riot and the political vampire cartoon I stumbled across in VCU's archives while researching "vampires in state politics" for my new horror film course. A few weeks before the Wilmington riot, the Raleigh *News & Observer* printed a large cartoon of a huge fanged Black vampire hovering over a ballot box and reaching his sharp claws out to five fleeing white voters, three of them women.

"The Vampire That Hovers Over North Carolina," depicted the vampire wearing a cape with the words "Negro Rule" on it. The cartoon appeared a year after Bram Stoker published *Dracula*, a trope that probably helped incite the riot weeks later. The effing takeaway—Blacks are sucking the life blood of whites, so suppress their votes!

Gathering data on dead white males, actually any dead people, creeps me out. Charlie Foxtrot to the 10th power!

March 27, 2019: Dr. Jackson Canaday

Dr. Humphrey introduced me to his colleague, Dr. Jackson Canaday, a young Assistant Professor of Political Science & Cultural Studies.

"Call me Jackson, not Doctor or Professor."

I smiled, thinking he was just a PhD, nothing else.

Grinning, he told us, "At a dinner party in my first year as a college teacher, a colleague's 11-year-old daughter asked me, 'What kind of doctor are you…the kind that makes people sick or makes them well?' That evening I jumped off my pedestal pretty fast."

Dr. Humphrey sipped his tea, frowned, and explained, "I hired Dr. Canaday to supervise and coordinate the interns as they do on-site cemetery research. With him as supervisor, I can visit Southern archive collections in Charleston, SC, and Marietta, GA, and expand our database."

After lunch, Dr. Humphrey left on an archival project to locate and visit a dozen or so large Southern cemeteries in Georgia for future VDP researchers. Jackson and I spent the next few hours going over local burial stats the interns had collected. At first, I couldn't tell how their data was different from the cemetery's public burial archives, which anyone could access.

Jackson pointed out their data went far beyond general public information in the cemetery archive. Interns recorded the length of time they stood before graves and the weather conditions of each visit, including temperature, wind velocity, and wind direction. They took readings of the decibel levels surrounding each grave, and estimated whether a group of three or four could simultaneously stand by the grave. Then standing before each grave's tombstone, they called Dr. Humphrey and left a 90-second blank message. The research team planned to collect data at each grave on different days at 9:00 am, 1:00 pm, and 6:00 pm. Overall, the VDP interns would conduct 5,400 grave interviews at Oakdale! Unfucking believable.

A bit stymied, I noticed some emerging patterns. All the dead listed are white males, born in the South, mostly in N.C. They were also 21 or older at the time of death, but who cares because now the youngest ones would be in their 70's. I must have been chewing my lower lip because Jackson asked, "Are you all right?"

"Yeah, these stats tell a story, but I'm not yet sure how to interpret them."

April 4, 2019: Jackson and Occam's Razor

Jackson and I met at the Riverview Cafe in Sneads Ferry, about 30 miles northeast of Wilmington. In the parking lot, he told me he grew up north of here, in Jacksonville, less than an hour up Highway 17 from Wilmington.

"So, you're a Cardinal, too?"

"How'd you know that?"

"Caden Cole, my old officemate at the University of Utah, was born and raised in Jacksonville. I even visited him there one Christmas."

"Damn…Junk Boy…talk about cosmic coincidence! He's a legend! Made me smile every time I saw him."

"Junk Boy?"

"Yep…that's what we called him. In his sophomore gym class, he wrestled another guy as two girls' exercise classes waited in the bleachers for Caden's class to end. He forgot to wear a jock and when his opponent cradled him for a pin, his boy toys exposed themselves.

"Coach Andy shouted across the gym, 'Cover your junk, boy!' From that moment on, he was 'Junk Boy.'"

Shaking my head, I smiled, "He never mentioned that in our Salt Lake City walks. Jeez, what could be worse for a kid?"

Jackson grinned, "To be called 'Little' Junk Boy!"

I nodded, "I agree." From then on, depending on circumstances, I knew I'd call Caden "LJB" instead of SOB or MOB.

The moment we entered the restaurant, I smelled fried okra and sweet onion hushpuppies. We both ordered sweet iced tea and stared out the window across the New River to Court House Bay and Camp Lejeune. Along the wharf were huge piles of netting and stacks of crab pots. One 3-person crew had just put up a "Fresh Shrimp for

35

Sale" sign for locals. Dozens of seagulls squawked and slowly circled the boats.

Jackson whispered, "I chose this place because I thought no one from Wilmington would be here. Sneads Ferry's a fishing village across the bridge from Camp Lejeune, the largest Marine Corps amphibian air base. The boats you see out the window are shrimp and crab boats, not tourist attractions."

When our food arrived, Jackson confessed as he broke a light brown hushpuppy into two pieces, "I sometimes get mixed messages from Dr. Humphrey. He's a good department head and distinguished scholar, but unaware or doesn't care about the bigger issues the VDP's pursuing. He's focused on retiring early and paying off his damn Albemarle 41, so he can take old rich Southern women on private tours. Right? Tours!" He popped half a hushpuppy into his mouth, and continued:

"Even so, he wants me to become department head after he retires. He's mentoring me through my tenure process and planning to retire two years after I'm tenured. He's relying on me to make his retirement a success. I couldn't ask for a more supportive colleague and mentor either. And like him, in four years with the VDP, I'll make enough extra money to put a down payment on a winter home for me and Jamie in Ashville."

Jackson paused, tipped his glass, and toasted, "Cheers to Dr. Humphrey."

He went on, "A couple of weeks ago it occurred to me what our goal really is. When Jamie got up in the middle of the night and left me alone in bed, I had an epiphany. Jesus, it's really simple, Occam's Razor...you know...William of Occam, the 14th century Franciscan friar?"

I nodded, and smiled because LJB named his electric razor "Occam" after a lecture we heard at the U of U on "The Principle of Simplicity." At Norfolk we called it K.I.S.S., "Keep It Simple, Stupid."

Jackson continued, "It's brilliant: grab the simplest explanation for something rather than create a complex interpretation. If it waddles like a duck, craps like a duck, and quacks like a duck, chances are it's an effing duck, not an alien or Mothman!

"Here's where I am now:

1. The VDP project focuses on known dead white male Southerners.

2. The current time line starts after the Civil War and ends with the Civil Rights Act, basically the Jim Crow era, spanning 101 years.

3. All our researchers and their subjects are white Southern men, excluding you.

4. We're confirming data already in each cemetery's burial records.

5. We're collecting new information which really has nothing to do with a dead person.

"So, using Occam's Razor, if we aren't verifying old data, what the hell are we doing? "VD" must mean something else.

"Is this making sense? I see a racially and gender-biased project that's going to cost hundreds of thousands, maybe millions, of dollars when it expands across the other Southern states with hundreds of cemeteries fitting the time frame. And we really don't know who's footing the bill for this project!"

I nod, "I still don't get why they're interested in this shit?"

I thought about Occam and smiled because Jackson was right. The answer is in front of us, but I can't see it. "If it's not the usual burial data they're after, what are they collecting and why?"

We sat silent for a few minutes looking across the bay. Jackson nodded and smirked as I poured ketchup over my fried okra, "As

Occam would point out, this project isn't about traditional graveside information...it's about each grave's environment!"

At 8:00, Jackson smiled at the last bite of his lemon meringue pie. I needed to drive back to Wilmington to look over the interns' latest burial statistics, get up early, and wander through Oakdale a few more times before heading north to Richmond. As I left the restaurant, Jackson told me, "Jamie and I live in Surf City on Topsail Island a few miles south of here, a small town with no Civil War monuments. We're not far from Ocean City, a historical Black community vacation resort, soon to become a part of the NC Civil Rights Trail. You might like the area.

"I'm going to stay a few more minutes and order a take home pecan pie for Jamie...and think about what we just said."

Caden's Comments

You turd merchant...Junk boy! I always thought Jackson smiled at me because I was cool, not the butt of a lingering joke.

I swigger, Ben will call me 'LJB' from now on in all his journal entries! What else did Ben learn from Jackson to heckle me with?

Why did the Council hire Ben to oversee research at two Southern cemeteries? This is creepier than a Guillermo del Toro horror film setting. Ben's reputation is his user-testing skills, not collecting data anyone can find.

Why did Jackson, who admires and trusts Humphrey, arrange a Sneads Ferry meeting with Ben for anonymity, why the focus on gravesite environments, and why does verifying this kind of data matter, and to whom? My head hurts as I wonder why Ben continued with the project.

Jackson wants Ben to apply Occam's razor to the data they're collecting. The fact Ben remembered I named my electric razor after Occam is awesome. I wasn't "Out of sight, out of mind."

38

I'm pretty sure Jamie was one of Jacksonville's High's blonde majorettes.

April 5, 2019: Why This Info?

In Wilmington, Jackson's words echoed in my mind. Oakdale stats started making sense. As new patterns emerged, I suspected my income was calling me. I ignored Occam like many U.S citizens do who follow media conspiracies playing on their economic fears. Jackson's observations almost made sense.

I still couldn't figure out why the Council of 5 called our research "the Verifying Data" Project. In this political climate which places low value on science and facts, who cares if dead people are "verified." Just look at their frigging graves! Our focus is on dead white men, and for what purpose? The bottom line is "What kind of Return on Investment will it bring project investors?"

I spent most of the week walking in Oakdale, reading historical markers, and looking at flower arrangements on graves. Every now and then I sat on a family memorial bench, read intern notes, and created graphic charts. This odd grave data was all I could think about as I toured Oakdale and enjoyed lightning bugs, crimson crepe myrtles, and bougainvillea branches swaying in the cool evening air. Questions buzzed around me like bees on the flowers around graves. The windborne whiffs reminded me of the scents in my parents' quarter-acre greenhouse.

Why the hell care about noise levels and wind speeds at each grave?

April 12, 2019: What Would Occam Think? (Lunch at Surf City, N.C.)

I gathered my travel gear and made sure my thumb drive contained the interns' files. It's a 5-hour drive to Richmond, but during our Sneads Ferry lunch Jackson convinced me to stop over in Jacksonville. His plan was good because I wasn't scheduled to meet the Richmond intern crew until the 15th. I'd have two days to visit some more places LJB told me about during our Salt Lake City and Seattle wanderings.

We met at a pizza place in Surf City on Topsail, perched on the edge of sand dunes protecting it from strong offshore winds. We were the only customers until a smiling elderly couple sat down shortly after we ordered. The owner took our order and smiled when I asked, "Do you have non-dairy cheese?"

With only two pieces of pizza left, Jackson leaned forward, "Bear with me here. Why does anyone care how many white men are buried in old cemeteries? Besides their descendants, who cares? And, secondly, they're dead…physically dead…in time turned into soil. OK, in your case as a plant-based person, it'd be organic soil. Even more important, why do we care now at this moment in U.S. history in 2019?"

He smiled, sipped his beer, "Like you said earlier, 'Why focus on burials from 1863 to 1964?' WWOT…What Would Occam Think?"

I looked out the window, watching a lone seagull hopping on the wet sand and sprays of foam blow off the surf and tumble down the beach. I asked myself, "Where's this increasingly loud outburst going?"

Jackson, his eyebrows raised, shook his head, looked around, and said, "Pretend you're a white male Southerner who died in 1875. What might you believe today?"

His forehead wrinkled, he raised his voice and continued, "You got it: the same as you believed then. The bottom line is this: today you'd still believe what you believed at your death!"

He tapped the table with his nearly empty beer mug; a few drops bounced onto his shirt, "And that's where Occam's Razor comes into play!"

The older well-dressed woman left her table during Jackson's outburst, walked across the room, and stood two tables from us, looking out the bay window as her husband took photos of her with the sandy beach and the surf in the background.

Jackson glanced at her, smiled, lowered his voice, "When we see data patterns of white deaths from the end of the Civil War through the Jim Crow era, why should we care about them? Why the "F" would we research them? And why does it matter if they were 21 or 31 at the time of their deaths? What matters is what they believe TODAY... which is what they believed then. Why the hell do we care what dead white men believe? And how do we know what they believe?

"What's scarier is how do we get living people to believe they can return to the old, dead, white male past?"

After a silent moment, we both shouted, "Social media!"

He grinned, "Yes! The best way to reinforce old beliefs today is through social media campaigns! Imagine how much money the Council of 5 would pay QAnon to divert us from the present by introducing weird ideas making the present less desirable and interesting than the past. Hell, we've already seen ideas like bad plots for graphic novels and computer games catch on and spread—Pizza Gate, fake news, witch hunts, the blame game, voter fraud, space alien interference, Lizard people, and the Holocaust and 9/11 never happened. Jesus. It's like shouting 'Squirrel' in front of your dog. The media loves it and thrives on it because people jump on these ideas and blame others for ignoring them and holding them back from realizing their vision of the past. We can only guess how much the media's income has grown since 2015. Jamie calls a salvo of social media finger-pointing a 'murmuration of tweets.'"

Jackson finished his beer and kept going, "These odd ideas reinforce binary thinking by pitting one idea against another, seldom recognizing a 3rd option, even if it's a combination of the first two. They reinforce accepted binary distinctions: Either/or, in/out, me/you, male/female, he/she, Republican/Democrat, good/bad, win/lose, rich/poor, socialism/democracy, Black/White, and in this case—living/dead.

"If you want to make an Antifa's head spin and their vision blur, just mention the word 'compromise' or the phrase 'social-democracy.' Use the pronoun 'They' instead of 'He or She.' Throw an 'and' instead of 'or' into the 'He/She' binary, jaws drop, and anger, based on fear, rises.

"Underlying all this binary thinking is the Toddler Tyrant's and our media's Blame Game like 'witch hunt,' and 'Obama is not a U.S. citizen.' It's a way of ignoring defeat, kind of a new version of the Lost Cause that retells the past as they want it to be, not as it was. Like the Lost Cause, these new narratives give people something to aspire to.

"The crazier the notion is, the more likely social media will play on it and attract emotional followers who seldom think critically. I'm pretty sure movers and shakers like Bernie Sanders, Alexandria Octavio-Cortez, and Stacey Abrams spend an inordinate amount of time and money on chiropractic adjustments from shaking their heads so damn much."

Jackson stopped, looked at the server, pointed at his beer mug, and continued, "According to Jamie, binary thinking favors a two-party political system, discourages compromise, and favors politics over people. Think about it: it's easy to play the political blame game if you have only two options, Democrats and Republicans. If you compromise, you're admitting other options exist. Hell, it's a first step towards Critical Thinking! Imagine if more politicians thought about all Americans rather than just people in their parties. Kind of a mind-blower."

Gunny Jones used to spew political advice to us outside the barracks at Pendleton. He once said, "Politicians and baby diapers should be changed often, and for the same reason." I sipped my beer and smiled.

The woman glanced at us as her husband twisted his wedding ring. A light flickered in my mind. What do these things have in common…the Jim Crow era, dead Confederate white men, and their antiquated unchanging thoughts?

I whispered, "Jesus, this project is a political strategy to make the past America's future. Of course, it's a stretch, but maybe VPD really is more than a deceptive, innovative way of looking backwards to 'Make America Great Again.' But how?"

Jackson slipped back deep into his bench, smiled, and raised his empty glass, "Spot on, Doctor Dunn." When the woman moved closer to us for a better landscape shot, he asked, "Ma'am, would you like me to take a photo of you and your husband?"

She smiled, "Why…yes, bless your heart, Suga'." While Jackson photographed them, I thought about what he just said. I stared at a dozen seagulls circling a slow-moving shrimper pulling in its nets a hundred yards or so offshore from the fishing pier. When Jackson returned to our table, I asked, "If VDP builds on dead people's responses, how the hell do you interview dead people?"

I had a flashback of the Wilmington interns leaving breakfast to help Yancey Jenkins conduct interviews. Jackson shook his head, "What are we missing?"

He looked at his blinking iPhone. "I've got to pick up some classy wine. It's our one-year anniversary. I want to get home with a chess pie, too, before Jamie does. Stop by for dinner when you get back from Richmond, and we'll brainstorm more about collecting and verifying data from dead folks. I know Jamie'd like to meet you.

"In the meantime, think about the new info we're gathering and how it fits into the 'Verifying Data' Project. Maybe you'll gather some more info from Hollywood Cemetery that'll help us see what Occam expects us to see."

The only car in the parking lot besides my rental Cayenne and Jackson's Honda Fit was a silver gull-wing Tesla. Jackson muttered, "They could have bought us dessert for taking so damn many photos. By the way, thanks for taking a few photos of me with them. Jamie'll love them. The photos of me, not the couple."

Caden's Comments

It's getting creepier. Occam is one of my heroes, so I'll follow his advice, even if no one else does. It's like Ben to support expanding the research time frame to generate more data and income.

Ben even questioned Return on Investments by the Council of 5. BCB still lives…at least in his journal entries.

Damn good point: social media and the Lost Cause! During my first year at VCU, I learned why Richmond is often called the "City of the Lost Cause." It's pretty obvious because Richmond was the Capital of the Confederacy, only 90 miles south of Washington, D.C., a brazen defiant Confederate act making the city the Capital of the South, sort of giving the North the finger.

A VCU librarian recommended I read Edward Pollard's 1867 book, *The Lost Cause: A New Southern History of the War of the Confederates*. Pollard, former editor of the *Richmond Times*, coined the term "the Lost Cause" and explained why holding on to past ideologies is important. But it was *Birth of a Nation*, D.W. Griffith's 1915 film that portrayed voting freed slaves as threats to contemporary Southern culture, especially white women, just as the *Raleigh Observer* vampire cartoon did. So, I know Jamie is right regarding media!

Griffith's film continued Pollard's myth and half a century later shows us how media spread the Lost Cause ideology by mythologizing the Southern defeat and viewing the past from a skewed white perspective. Both the writer and the filmmaker convinced many Southerners in the Jim Crow era that slavery was just an honorable process providing jobs and care for displaced Black people, who were happy working for their masters…really their owners.

Crap, I can't imagine what the U.S. would be like today if social media had been alive at the turn of the 20th century. How many FB hits would Griffith's film have gotten today?

Wise strategy, Jackson…applying Occam to cultural and political binary thinking! Binary thinking is something I regularly discuss with students. By the end of the semester, I like watching my students become more in-depth critical thinkers, impressed by how they critique social media campaigns, find the truth in posted articles, and question web domains and their extensions. Eventually they rely more on '.gov., .edu., and .org.' than on '.com. and .net.'

Even better, they question the data they're reading, the qualifications of the people who provided it, and credibility of the website. They teach me something every day in class. It's fun to watch them thump binaries on the nose and turn into critical thinkers quicker than a young person bitten by a vampire turns into one.

Last spring semester, an undergrad called out my class for attacking social media. They said, "I call it the 'hoe effect.' You can use your garden hoe to plant roses or kill your friends, if they threaten you. In either case, the decision on how to use it is yours, not the hoe's or social media's."

Not bad, blaming the user not the product. I wonder if they belong to the NRA? The 'Hoe Theory' gives new meaning to "stand your ground." There'll probably be an uptick in hoe deaths, too!

It took the weekend for Aslyn, my teaching assistant at the time, to calm down. But in Monday's class she substituted "guns" for "hoes" and showed her students how to inform themselves with statistical data. She asked half the class to visit a few websites and see how many people died by gun violence in the past three years in the U.S. She asked the other half to find how many people died from garden implements. On Wednesday the class listened to each group's findings, and she introduced fear, mass murder, school shootings, and social history into the narrative.

Aslyn pointed out to them, "Changing the trope from hoes to guns changes our views of reality and forces us to confront our personal beliefs and their impact on society." The class had an amazing discussion of binary and systemic thinking and its effect on our personal political acts, including voting.

Unexpectedly, in the last few minutes, one student asked the class, "What do you think it'll take for politicians to look at gun death data and do something about it?"

One student, the only parent, a father of four, said, "Our data shows, it's not gonna be the number of kids killed."

After a few moments of silence, one young woman blurted, "Tourism! Our group learned from the trade.gov website that international visitors spend more than half a billion dollars a day in the U.S. So, when international visitors are scared shitless and quit visiting our country and our income drops, Congress will finally pull its head out of its bi-partisan ass, and change the laws to save money, not people!"

Everyone clapped as class ended.

After class, I bought Aslyn a "thank you" Diet Dr. Pepper, her favorite drink.

I recalled Jamie's comments on blurred binaries and thought about my students' binary discussions in my disability classes. We never know when illness, disease, or an accident will compromise our bodies and minds, and when we'll need an "accommodation," one of the most contentious terms in the 1990 American with Disabilities Act (ADA). "Accommodation" often angered businesses and able-bodied people when customers requested "expensive" accommodations. Research shows building steps, accessible entrances, and parking spaces cost a small amount to make sure every customer can visit their business to buy their products and increase their sales. Even so, fearing the unexpected costs, many businesses put accommodations on the back burner.

Face it: Our bodies are in flux, changing in unexpected ways. But we systemically ignore our changing bodies and assume we either have a body without a disability or a body with one. Some of us live with episodic disabilities, you know, the kind that flair up and disappear unexpectedly like seizures. We seldom think about our needing an accommodation until we get pregnant, injured, ill, or old. Even so, some of us will never need an accommodation. Historically, as a nation we've basically seen "accommodations" as bothersome acts of charity, something we do to help a "special" group and make us feel good, too. Jesus! The 2008 ADAA takeaway: binaries change, just as we sometimes do.

So, could binaries shift in other ways? Could other binaries also be in flux and need us to rethink them? Could a Democrat vote Republican and vice versa? Could vampires and zombies be popular culture metaphors for blurred binaries? Damn straight!

April 13, 2019: Jacksonville, N.C. (Marine Memorial)

I arrived in Jacksonville around 4:30, just in time to hit base traffic from Camp Lejeune. On Jackson's recommendation I stayed at Hilton's Home2 Suites off Western Boulevard in the middle of a series of strip shopping complexes and restaurants continuing for several miles. If it's a chain store, it's probably in this area from the Olive Garden to the Golden Corral, perfect for a city whose average age is around 23. A host of small Italian, Greek, Thai, and Indian restaurants dot the strip. Hell, LJB could find vegan items in most places.

The next morning, I placed a bouquet of tulips and roses on LJB's parents' graves. They're buried in their family plot, shaded by two large purple crepe myrtles, where most Coles had been buried since the 1930s. Surprised at the cemetery's burial contract, LJB told me it read, "No people of color will be buried in this cemetery for time immemorial."

He later confessed, "I wish I'd known this before making funeral arrangements, but I knew Mom wanted to be buried beside her parents and siblings." He felt compromised, and wondered if his parents had ever seen the contract, signed by his great grandfather.

Across the highway from the city cemetery was one of LJB's most talked about places: the Montford Point Marine Memorial, a site honoring Black Marines, a Viet Nam War Memorial, and the

Beirut Memorial. Montford was originally the segregated boot camp for Black Marines barred from Parris Island, S. C., boot camp from 1942 until 1949. LJB was pleased his dad, a Gulf War vet, could see from his grave shaded by pine and oak trees the community-sponsored memorial across the highway.

I spent nearly two hours walking around statues, viewing photos, and reading bronze descriptions of the Black Marines' contributions. I learned the history of Montford Point, now Camp Johnson named after Sgt. Major Gilbert "Hashmark" Johnson, a highly decorated Black Marine, and one of the first African American drill instructors. I wondered why no teacher, especially in this area, ever told LJB and his classmates about the WWII Pacific contributions to our country by more than 20,000 Black Marines.

All I could think about was Critical Race Theory, *The 1619 Project*, and how our culture whitewashes our real history and sometimes keeps new information invisible. I remembered Caden telling me, "In the Jim Crow era, when white schools in many coastal Carolina counties received new books with updated information, administrators often gave their outdated textbooks to Black schools. They felt good about passing on their books to Black schools even though the information was a decade or so old. Hardly anyone listened to teachers' complaints that outdated information kept Black students from succeeding on college entrance exams."

Placed into perspective, I saw the need for the Montford Point Marine Memorial and updating real historical information. I imagined LJB's dad smiling at Marines from across the highway. I heard them all yelling, "Semper Fi!" I whispered, "Semper Fi," saluted, and walked back to my rental in the parking lot.

After leaving Montford Point, I stopped at Brewed Downtown, one block away, the coffee shop LJB took us to both days during my visit. I ordered a takeout dairy-free mocha, turned down Stratford Road, which abutted Montford Point, and drove just over a mile through LJB's neighborhood to Wilson Bay Park, where he spent most of his childhood. I walked out on the small dock, and looked across the bay, imagining LBJ and his buds on an alligator hunt in a cheap rental row boat.

When I finished my mocha, I drove down New Bridge Street to the New Bridge Organic Market, picked up some vegan snacks, and headed back to the Home2 Suites.

Under my door were business cards from two different women wanting to know if I needed "evening company" while in town. The next morning, tired from entertaining, I began my 230-mile jaunt to the Holiday Inn in downtown Richmond.

Caden's Comments

I'm pleased Ben remembered so much about the two days we spent in Jacksonville, especially little things like gator hunting. I knew he'd like Montford Point. There are few places where three memorials honor Marines at the same time. My parents really liked Ben, especially Dad, who'd be happy he visited their graves. I'm sending him a cosmic thanks for dropping by to see them and probably saluting my dad. I know we could never have visited Ben's dad's grave together. If we had, I'm sure Ben would have urinated on it.

Even though I'm enjoying these journal entries, it still pisses me off to be called LJB.

April 15, 2019: Richmond, VA

Last spring, when I visited LJB at Virginia Commonwealth University, I stayed at the Holiday Inn across from his studio apartment in a high-rise on Cary Street. Hollywood Cemetery was a just a few blocks from LJB's office on the main VCU campus. One night after class we sneaked over to check out the Richmond Vampire legend. LJB was introducing vampires to his film class on "Monsters, Fear, and Our Neighborhoods" and felt local lore best proves his point: vampires and monsters in general are tropes for our economic fears caused by the wealthy sucking the blood of workers. For three hours we sat under a blooming magnolia with two six packs and our flashlights. We saw no vampires, not even a stray cat. We planned to see the Byrd Theater's 48 Hour Horror Film Festival in October, but my new consulting schedule shot down that meet up.

LJB now lives in an exclusive townhouse, across the James River, about six miles from campus. It's a damn shame I can't stay at his place. We'd have a ball wandering around Richmond, munching and sipping our way through bars in Shockoe Slip, the Fan District, and Carytown. We'd visit the small Edgar Allen Poe Museum, the Museum of the Confederacy, the Virginia Museum of Contemporary Art, and walk through Caden's new neighborhood not far from the river's edge.

Richmond is large enough I can avoid running into LJB during my short stay. I knew he avoided Hollywood in the day and only visited it at night with small groups of graduate students during Halloween week.

The Council of 5 selected Hollywood because it's the resting place for about 11,000 known Confederate soldiers. Following the VDP's directive for grave visits, the interns will need around 33,000 grave site visits.

Tomorrow I'm scheduled to meet Yancey Jenkins, the head MAGA interviewer, at a bistro in the Fan District not far from Hollywood.

April 16, 2019: Yancey Jenkins' Survey Questions for Discarnates

A tourist brochure at the hotel told me Hollywood is a 135-acre garden cemetery. Its beauty earned it official designation as an arboretum. Founded several years before the Civil War, Hollywood became the burial place of more than 11,000 Confederate soldiers. Richmond, as Capital of the Confederacy, established its historical link to the "Lost

Cause" just as Fort Fisher deaths and Wilmington's 1898 riot made Oakdale another perfect site for the VD Project.

Other than me, the only person to appear at both Oakdale and Hollywood cemeteries is Yancey Jenkins. He summoned the interns in Wilmington to help him at the first graveside interview several weeks ago.

In a Google search, I learned Jenkins was a Richmond disability lawyer and CPA, who grew up near Todd, N.C., a small Appalachian community famous for its UFO sightings. He was a prosecutor who worked with mediums to solve murders. Police departments all over the South contacted him to solve cold murder cases. A medium himself, he learned valuable information from holding items touched by the deceased.

He later founded the CPA, the Confederate Psychic Association, and assigned mediums to Southern families wanting to know more about their dead relatives buried in Confederate cemeteries. Families provided him with heirloom keepsakes, usually Bibles and photographs, but often mourning rings containing relative's ashes or hair, or other items their loved ones had touched. His fees were quite high, much higher than Ancestor.com.

Maybe Jackson was right again. Mediums conducting interviews in Southern cemeteries appeal to the Council of 5's desires, but why? As soon as I entered the small cafe in Carytown, a trim good-looking guy spotted me, walked over, and smiled, "Something tells me you're Ben Dunn!"

Not too impressive for a medium because I was the only effing customer in the cafe. He introduced himself, as "Yancey Jenkins, VDP's Interview Supervisor." I wanted to ask if he was a PDh, but I didn't.

We ordered a light lunch—sweet iced tea, a Cobb salad for him, a vegan salad for me, and biscuits. He asked me to call him "Yancey." I smiled, "Ben." He ordered a small bowl of Grandma's Molasses to dip our biscuits in.

During our chat, Yancey told me, "We held our first full-scale interview at Oakdale Cemetery in Wilmington last week. It didn't go as we'd hoped. The interns' data was flawed. Since Dr. Humphrey never showed them how to record their data, they were confused and fudged some of the answers for their report. The interviews also didn't go well either because the four of us couldn't fit around six of the ten graves I'd selected."

He rambled on, "Disappointed, Dr. Humphrey reassigned his interns to a community project at Fort Fisher, a short drive from Oakdale. Fort Fisher is the Southern Gibraltar, famous as one of the most decisive battles in N.C. when it was captured by the Union in 1865. Most of its dead are buried in Oakdale Cemetery."

Although I wanted to, I didn't ask Yancey why Humphrey shifted the interns to a fortification site, not another cemetery. I must have looked confused because Yancey said, "Dr. Humphrey didn't tell you about the results of our interviews either, did he?"

"No, he didn't." I wondered where this chat was going and wanted to see the former interns' data templates.

"Our Richmond team so far has gathered data on about 200 graves. This week we'll conduct 20 interviews daily until we have a solid data base for future remote interviews. Of course, everything depends on how we define 'death.'"

I must have still looked confused because Yancey asked, "You do know I'm a psychic, and my interviews must be conducted in person near the discarnate's grave and continuing presence?"

Nodding, I thought about interviews at the discarnate's grave and their continuing presence! Dude, just say the "living dead." I knew Jackson would approve of Yancey's ignoring the life/death binary.

"Our bosses hired me a year ago to replace the research project submitted by the NRA and rejected by the Council."

I blurted, "The National Rifle Association?"

"No, no, not the National Rifle Association," he smiled as he dipped the last biscuit into the bowl of molasses.

"The National Resurrection Alliance, a group of secret psychic researchers based in Atlanta. They proposed to resurrect all Confederate veterans and their sons, just weeks before a Presidential election and have them vote through certified surrogates who'll fill out their ballots for them. Sort of builds on the fake news that Democrats used dead voters to rig elections."

"Voting…my ass!" I thought.

Yancey looked around, paused, wiped a spot of molasses off his chin, and rambled on, "The NRA's return on the Council's investment was absurd. They planned to raise zombie voters, contain them as detainees in immigration detention centers along Texas and Louisiana borders, take them to poll sites, and rebury them or what was left of them after the election.

"The NRA didn't focus on the expense of resurrecting zombies, containing them for community safety, transporting them, probably at night in government vehicles to and from their graves to the voting polls, and then paying for their reinternment.

"Not only would such a proposal cost millions of dollars. Even more disturbing, the NRA couldn't tell who their zombies would vote for. Their researchers knew nothing about the discarnate voters except for information they found in public cemetery records. They had no backup safety protocols in their proposal.

"And they were NOT tech savvy! They proposed to put GPS trackers on each zombie to track them after leaving the detention centers. It never occurred to them, how much it would cost to retrieve a lost rotting limb containing the device and then search for the missing zombie.

"The NRA never even considered the public's reaction if zombies wandered off the immigration centers into neighborhoods and shopping centers, littering streets and sidewalks with rotting body parts. The cost of body part retrieval is staggering! Worse yet, the zombie demographic could vote only once before rotting away!

"My proposal costs a small fraction of the NRA's. We focus only on the spiritual, not the physical body. There are no transportation or detainee costs, parts to recover, or threats to neighborhoods. So far, we've spent less than $50,000—mostly on cell phones, lunches for our unpaid college interns, travel expenses, and my salary.

"Our information comes from discarnate voters themselves, not public cemetery records. Interviewees tell us the kind of President they want based on their past preferences. Since our discarnate voters live in their past, we can count on their votes to reflect their past beliefs in every future Presidential election. We will only register voters whose past is our future."

Yancey's graveside interviews made sense to me from an ROI perspective, if nothing else. Damn! His salary must be only around $100 an hour. I hope nobody's told him my salary, which would probably send him and his program to another group of investors, some weird-ass dark corporate group. In my case, silence is literally golden!

An hour later, we met his interns, each from a different Richmond college, at Hollywood. Based on public grave information, Yancey knew the best graves for the interview team, who needed space for a family keepsake, his folding camp chair, and a recording intern. The other two interns stood nearby holding large studio umbrellas, protecting the site from eavesdroppers, distracting flashing lights, wind, and muffling outside noise caused by traffic during the interviews.

Yancey asked each discarnate the same questions to determine data patterns and gravesite efficiency, his description of "verifying data." Using Dr. Humphrey's suggestions, Yancey developed a simple questionnaire requiring only a "Yes or No" response. My mind drifted to Occam. I felt data screaming, "Ben! Ben!"

Yancey continued, "My simple poll almost guarantees data trends we can easily verify."

I listened while he read the latest version of his questionnaire:

"1. Were you born in the South?

2. Were you 21 or older when you left your body?

3. Are you male?

4. Are you white?

5. Have you ever voted?

6. Do you want to vote?

7. Have you learned anything new since you became "disabled?"

8. Do you wish to preserve the America you or your ancestors fought for?

9. Do you want a white male U.S. President?"

Damn, I never saw this coming! Now I understood why the Council hired me. As weird as Yancey's questions were, all I could think about was how he user-tested them. His questionnaire needed beta testing before his next round of interviews. I wondered who he tested his interview template on before launching it on "discarnates." I'd bet Dr. Humphrey's large wrinkled white ass if Yancey user-tested his questionnaire, he tried it out only on living white male college interns. My inner nerd rose because I get so excited over beta testing. Hell, I'm even using the word "discarnate" instead of "dead."

"Why do you use only 'yes/no' questions in your survey?"

Yancey smiled, "I'm basing my questions on electronic voice phenomenon (EVP) research. For years parapsychologists have interpreted many sounds on recordings as spirit voices. One famous parapsychologist felt spirit sounds were brief, the reason we wanted 'Yes' or 'No' responses.

"But are they really brief, short sounds or maybe units of compressed information? What if a short noise is really a ten-minute chat or explanation smashed into a one-second blurb? We make a 90-second call from each grave to give discarnates time to leave a message and for us to record the sound. Maybe our technology just can't pick it up yet! For now, we're just assuming a short noise equals a short response from discarnates until we learn more."

Jackson is right: use Occam's Razor, and look for the obvious. The VD or Verifying Data Project really is the "Verifying Deaths Project," a strategy where discarnate interviews, death, and disabled come together. It's mind-boggling that "disabled" links to "discarnate." I looked forward to meeting with Jackson in Sneads Ferry next week to sort all this out.

Before one of the largest family graves with "Major, CSA" carved after the discarnate's name, Yancey opened his camp chair, sat down, held his cell to his right ear, and closed his eyes. The interns crowded around him, pencils in hand. He whispered, "Please turn off your cell phones." He worried intern voices and phone sounds might confuse or distract the discarnate who must concentrate on Yancey's voice as he asked interview questions.

I stood outside the circle and muttered to myself as Yancey spoke and frequently nodded his head. He and the interns conducted twenty more 10-minute interviews at different graves and then fist-bumped before gathering their props.

As we walked through Hollywood, Yancey pointed out some "Lost Cause" sites like the graves of Confederate supporter U.S. President John Tyler, General George Pickett, known for Pickett's Charge at Gettysburg, and Jefferson Davis, President of the Confederate States of America. He talked fast and glanced around trying to figure out which grave to visit first.

Yancey spread his hands, pointed his palms upwards, looked at me with tears in his eyes, "Isn't this amazing!" He stopped near

General George Pickett's grave, wiped his eyes with his sleeve, and muttered, "If everyone had just listened to them!"

Later, driving out of the cemetery, I remembered Richmond is the site of a number of contentious Civil War statues on Monument Avenue, not far from VCU. During our discussions, Yancey never mentioned the Richmond Vampire, an omission that would've pissed off LJB.

Over the next four days, I met Yancey by numerous graves in Hollywood and watched him and his interns interview 80 more discarnates. To tourists we probably looked like a group of white men quietly honoring the Confederate dead, which in an odd way was true.

I spent my last two days in Richmond alone, reviewing interview notes, and analyzing the responses for data patterns. On the next day, Yancey dropped off lunch from his favorite takeout in Shockoe Slip. When I opened the bag, there was only a soft-shelled crab Po' Boy sandwich in it. The bar must have given him somebody's else's order. Damn, when I tasted it, it was amazing! I drove down to Shockoe that night and gorged on soft-shelled crabs.

After dinner, I visited the Virginia Museum of Fine Arts and drooled over their collection of Fabergé eggs. Because the Museum of the Confederacy was moving to another Richmond location farther away from the Medical College of Virginia campus, I couldn't see the thunder mugs LJB told me about.

Instead of coffee mugs with sketches of Confederate memorabilia or small antique cannons, Caden once emailed me photos of several Confederate chamber pots, another type of thunder mug, a well-named one I might add. At the bottom of these pots were drawings of Lincoln or Grant, so the Confederate user could assault his enemies with his own fecal matter. "Thunder" was a good word to describe the sound of the process.

I knew this idea was a moneymaker in today's political climate, so I pitched a scenario, "Caden, imagine how much you could make if you started a side business selling stickers with waterproof photos of POTUS and Congress members from both sides of the aisle. Anyone could purchase a few decals and stick them in their toilets or urinals to express their political views. In a year, you could pay off your damn townhouse."

I knew LJB wouldn't follow up, so I started my own anonymous company, "Vent Your Views!" and made $40,000 my first quarter. We sold three times as many photos of Democrats than Republicans. But sales demographics are changing because more young people are registering to vote, many as Independents.

I wished I could drop by LJB's office, and see his new townhouse, but I had to stay invisible for my salary and job perks.

Reading over my interview notes, I saw the questionnaire as grossly inadequate. The interview questions made sense to Yancey and his interns, but maybe not to discarnates. The questions must be user-tested on discarnates and revised based on their responses before Yancey can launch a wide-scale interview protocol and present his data to the Council. Even though each interview question required a binary "Yes/No" response, the one odd thing sticking out was question #7: "Have you learned anything new since you became 'disabled?'"

This question reminded me of a lecture on disability rhetoric LJB delivered at a conference held at the U. He told the audience that disability terminology changes as we rethink the use of "disability." Yancey just assumed his interviewees understood what "disabled" means in 2019. "Disabled" didn't become a common American word until after WWII. During the Civil War, wounded soldiers who wanted to help their country joined the Invalid Corps, which later became the Reserves. So, words like "invalid," "handicapped," and "disabled" reflect the changing times, limited to a specific generation. Terms for people with disabilities often reflected a negative patronizing cultural view of people seen as ranging from "survivors or overcomers" to "unworthy," not as people. Answering "Yes or "No" to #7 is a mind stretch, especially for older discarnates. Moreover, #7 is the only question expecting a "No" response.

Intern notes showed each discarnate took longer to answer this question than all of the others combined. "Disabled" confused post-Civil War discarnates because historically in the U.S. "disabled," meant among other things, "defective." I'll suggest to Yancey and Dr. Humphrey to make question #7 a more relevant, recognizable, and less confusing word for each generation of discarnates, depending on their death dates. Or better yet, use "Dead" for "Disabled" in #7 for wounded Confederate veterans.

User testing rules! I'm finally earning my salary! Hell, I'm even sounding like a PhD, not a PDh!

Caden's Comments

You codpiece! You ate an effing crab! What is it about veganism you don't get! So, you were vegan only when I was around? How'd I miss that? I wonder how many of the meals you mention in this damn journal are really vegan scams!

Hell, he liked me enough to change his diet around me so I'd be comfortable. Even so, we still needed a longer chat on the long-range environmental impact of veganism.

I wish I could have toured Hollywood with Ben and Yancey. I'd love to have seen Yancey's face when I told them about Pickett's connection with Bellingham during the "Pig War" in the Strait of San Juan de Fuca in the Pacific Northwest.

In 1859 Pickett was the Union Captain who led a group of American soldiers onto San Juan Island to protect the area from the British as the "Pig War" escalated. Fortunately, no one except the pig was injured or killed. (But for a hard-core vegan a dead pig causes a moment of sad silence). Following orders, Pickett built a fort to protect the area and a bridge over Squalicum Creek in Bellingham just a few yards from the current downtown Post Office and a few blocks from my apartment.

In 1861 Pickett resigned from the Union army and became the General in the Confederate army, who led the famous Pickett's Charge at the Battle of Gettysburg. In 1917, the local chapter of the Daughters of the Revolution named the Bellingham bridge, "The Pickett Bridge." A hundred years later, shortly after the Charlottesville, VA., white supremacy riot in 2017, the Bellingham City Council removed Pickett's name from the memorial bridge.

I can't imagine the reactions of Yancey and the Charlottesville rioters if someone told them General Pickett's second wife was Morning Mist, an indigenous Haida woman from the area, who tragically died giving birth to their son. Yancey's whitewashed spin on this seldom mentioned fact would be mind-boggling.

How would Yancey react if he heard me tell the interns that in 1990 Virginia's Douglas Wilder, a Democrat, became the first Black Governor in U.S. history?

Smiling, I wonder how often Ben visited Bellingham and if he actually dropped off the Mystery Box before his murder.

It never occurred to me immigrant centers might just be a secret social media campaign to contain Confederate zombies and keep them invisible, sort of a diversion from the NRA's true purpose: to make detention centers voting sites for zombies. Now I get why many southern states and the current administration support the border wall and the immigrant camps so effing much!

Didn't the NRA see that a hoard of zombies might play on public fear of a coming apocalypse? They should watch a season of *The Walking Dead* to see zombie impact on communities. Of course, characters in *iZombie* and *Post Mortem* are working on cures for zombies and vampires. Maybe the NRA is focusing now on medical scientific facts, not on false rumors of apocalyptic fear spawned by film and popular culture. It's moments like this when I know teaching horror film is necessary and a godsend.

I wonder if Yancey knows about Joe Dante's *Homecoming*. After dead Iraqi war vets come home to the U.S., they rise from their coffins and graves and lurch to voting booths to overturn the next election and prevent the Bush party from sending citizens to fight and die in a meaningless war. At the film's end, vets from all U.S. wars rise to vote and end political stupidity. Voting zombies are not new to the satiric horror film world.

Yancy went one step further than Dante with his focus on discarnate spirits, not on discarnate bodies. Pretty progressive thinking. Maybe Aslyn and I can show *Homecoming* and see how our students might outline its sequel.

I can hardly wait to get Aslyn's take on Jim Crow zombies walking through small towns. They'd become unimaginably aggressive if they encountered a young Black boy drinking from a public water fountain at a drug store, a Black and white couple sitting on a park bench with their baby in a stroller, or a gay couple kissing at a bus stop before one of them got on the bus. I'm sure she'd ask her students to write the opening scenes for a movie based on these encounters.

How the hell did I forget Ben's Thunder Mug proposal? I often wondered how he suddenly got enough money to gift me $40,000 for a townhouse. I'd have been pleased to vent my personal views. I knew BCB was on to something, but teaching distracted me and I dumped the project.

CADEN'S QUEST CONTINUES
(OCTOBER 2, 2020 TO NOVEMBER 17, 2020)

CHAPTER 6:
CADEN SEEKS HELP
(OCTOBER 2, 2020)

S itting outside Cafe Kaffeine, Caden realizes he needs local help with his research on Ben so he can still work on his sabbatical project. M.J. immediately comes to mind because she impressed him with her memory and finesse as well as her general looks. He peeks over the *Herald*, watches her come out, clear tables, and slip tips into the back pocket of her tight-fitting slacks as she leans over to clean a table across from him.

He tells his cell, "Interview M.J. asap and run it by Aslyn." Caden goes inside, orders another mocha, and stops beside M.J. "When is it the least busy here?"

M.J. nods, "As you see, you can socially distance easily in here, so don't worry about it. Usually Tuesday afternoons around 3:00 aren't busy, probably our quietest time."

On the next Tuesday, he meets her on break at an outside table during the day's drizzle. From about eight feet away, he introduces himself, "I'm Caden Cole, an English Professor at Virginia Commonwealth University here on a sabbatical project. I'm searching for a local person to help me research an online project. What are you majoring in, and would you be interested in working for me?"

She smiles, "I'm Melody Johnson, M.J., as most people know me. I just graduated from WWU's Fairhaven College and focused on law and diversity. I'm waiting for Covid to slow so I can start law school at the University of Washington. I plan to be a non-profit lawyer focused on regenerative farming and eliminating community food deserts."

He's hooked and hopeful. He wonders if she's a vegan. He tells her, "I'm trying to solve a year-old local murder and learn more about 'The VD Project,' a national project of sorts." She turns her head to the side and studies him, probably wondering if he's crazy.

"You won't have to quit being a barista. I need only four hours weekly. Until mid-January, I'll pay $120 weekly for three hours of research, and a weekly one-hour Zoom meeting. Text me by Monday if you want to audition for the job, and we'll arrange our first Zoom chat."

He picks up his mocha, walks off, turns, and shouts, "By the way, 'VD' means 'Verifying Data.'" M.J. looks relieved, the other two outside customers less so.

He calls Aslyn that night. Tyrone answers, "Everything is chill, doc." Laughing, he yells, "It's Doc Caden, your mentor, honey girl."

"Mentor, my ass!" she screams back. She picks up the phone and sees Tyrone had left the speaker on. Caden heard everything she had said. He notices she is politer than usual, "Hey, Doc Caden…what's happening? See any people of color this week?"

He waits and then cuts to the chase, "My old friend Ben Dunn was murdered, and I need your help to find his killer."

A long silence follows, and he hears Aslyn breathe deeply, "I'm so sorry, Doc. I know how close you two were. I know he disappeared, but murder never occurred to me. What can we do for you?"

Over the next half hour, he fills her in. "I'm not sure his disappearance and murder are related, but I need to know if a connection exists." He tells her about M.J. and his job audition offer. Another long silence follows.

"I need someone from this area, specifically Whatcom County, to help me locate info about Ben. I'm sending you M.J.'s resumé. Let me know your thoughts."

Tyrone shouts in the background, "RIPA! Run It Past Aslyn. That's what I do!"

An hour later he receives an email from M.J. wanting to audition for his offer. She asks him for a list of topics to research and wonders if they could Zoom next Tuesday at 7:00 p.m. He responds, "Absolutely."

His topic list is small, but important, "I need more personal info about Ben Dunn, August Humphrey, Jackson Canaday, and now Yancey Jenkins. Biographical background information is important to see if they have any connections beyond the VDP. I'm particularly interested in why Ben was murdered."

He explains Occam's Razor and says, "Look out for the obvious because we often fail to see it."

CHAPTER 7:
BEN LIVED AT POINT ROBERTS, WA
(OCTOBER 6, 2020)

f M.J. were one of his students, she'd earn an "A" for her research skills. What she's found so far makes him edgy.

According to a small independent gillnetter M.J. knows, "Ben identified as Nate Benjamin, a professional photographer. He moved to Point Roberts in early 2019, lived alone in a pricey beach condo and seldom went out in public. His passion in life was wildlife photography, and he often left the Point to catch planes in Vancouver, B.C."

She tells him, "Point Roberts, WA, is one of the oddest and most beautiful places in Whatcom County. Geologists call it a pene enclave. It's not physically attached to Whatcom County, but a bottom part of Tsawwassen, British Columbia, with fewer than 1,000 residents, dwindling because of the pandemic. Although physically attached to Canada, it's legally part of the U.S. The Point is quiet and beautiful and a pain in the butt for U.S. residents to get to. If you drive 94 miles roundtrip from Bellingham to Point Roberts, you have to cross the border four times."

He can't imagine now much time you have to wait in line at each border crossing. Even though the pandemic closed down the border in March 2020, Caden knows if Ben were alive, he'd still find The Point appealing.

When Caden asks how she found Ben's name, she says, "Since you both like playing with codes, I figured he'd use a simple version of his name, like many people do with their passwords. So, I played around with 'Benjamin Nathan Dunn,' and finally stumbled over the name of a recent Point Roberts resident in an internet search, 'Nathan Benjamin.' I found no direct link between Ben's obituary and Nate Benjamin, but since 'Nate/Nathan' doesn't appear after July, 2019, I assume both people are the same person.

"'Nathan' spent most of his time alone. But several people thought he was having an affair with his condo's new assistant manager. Each person had seen them walking on the beach or on trails holding hands. All of them described her as a 'blonde knockout.'"

M.J. discovered "Nathan" had flown to Martha's Vineyard twice, and to Wilmington, N.C. several times. Since he never mentioned Ben's flights, he knows she's on to something. Her audition over, he hires her to research until he leaves in mid-January.

"Send me your notes and I'll send you a weekly set of questions until I head back to Virginia. Even if we don't have one, I'll pay you for a weekly Zoom meeting."

Smiling, he emails a copy of M.J.'s findings to Aslyn as an FYI or as he now calls it, a RIPA.

CHAPTER 8:
OUR ZOOM UPDATE
(OCTOBER 17, 2020)

Aslyn waved as he clicked on the Zoom icon, "Hey, Doc Caden! Happy almost Halloween!"

"Happy almost Halloween to you and Tyrone, too."

She grinned. "Glad you could make it! Just want to update you on our 'Disability in the Horror Film' course and thank you for assigning it to me. It's fun watching my class discuss the connections between disfigurement and horror film monsters in pre-2000 films.

"Yesterday, I introduced horror monsters as common metaphors for people with disabilities. Our Zoom groups are exploring disfigurement in particular and disability in general. Freddy Kruger's and Michael Myers' disfigurements visually distance viewers from the bad guys. Talk about building on old cultural stereotypes. On your suggestion, we checked out *Nosferatu*, the 1922 silent vampire film, and realized disfigurement and monsters have played on our screens for nearly a century."

Caden reminded her to share with her class Chicago's 1881 Ugly Law, which forbade people with repulsive disabilities, often poor beggars, from using city streets.

Aslyn continued, "I just showed *The White Zombie,* the first zombie film produced in 1932, the same year as Tod Browning's *Freaks* and only a year after his *Dracula.* Vampires, zombies, and characters with disabilities entered our media almost intertwined. In *The White Zombie* Black people became enslaved zombie mill workers to bring more wealth to Haitian landowners. It reeks of the Lost Cause.

"Of course, nobody cared about zombies because they were all Black and socially invisible. But when a beautiful young white woman was purposely turned into one, things changed. After this first week, I think the class is hooked and ready to dive deeper into the not-so-subtle use of disability, sexism, and racism in later horror films."

Caden told her, "Next week I'll send you my notes on vampires and porphyria, a national news media focus in the late '80s. As usual, news coverage took over everything else, and this was before social media and daily tweets.

"A Canadian professor read a paper at a 1985 scientific conference showing a historical link between people living with porphyria, a rare inherited disorder, and vampires. News networks jumped on the fact that both vampires and people with porphyria shared similar behaviors such as avoiding sunlight. Media linked porphyria patients with vampires, and their painful and sometimes life-threatening disorder became the butt of cruel jokes.

"For nearly five years, whenever news reporters talked about the rare painful disease with doctors, pictures of Bela Lugosi and other vampires flitted across the screen behind them. By 1990 after the ADA became the law, media pulled back on its vampire coverage. I can't imagine the embarrassment people with porphyria and their families felt because they appeared as monsters and jokes in their communities. I'm still researching the lingering emotional impact of that media coverage. When I return to VCU, I'll share what I've learned."

Tyrone quietly moved behind Aslyn holding a Diet Dr. Pepper for her.

She shook her head, and continued, "Damn, Doc. This disease coverage plays well into my course. We Black folks catch shit like this whenever someone finds one of us has vitiligo. As Jerome usually says, 'Social media is Charlie Foxtrot to the nth power!'"

Jerome put Aslyn's drink down, pointed his index fingers in the air, twirling them, moving side to side, and shaking his head. Asyln interrupts, "That's Tyrone's clusterfuck dance."

"Hey, I'm following your syllabus, and adding a few twists to make it mine. We're discussing zombies as a way of perceiving death and critiquing materialism and capitalism. We started with Romero's *Dawn of the Dead*, and are applying Occam's razor to mall customers—in this case zombies. Every evening I turn towards the West and send good thoughts to Jordan Peele, who really helps me express what I've felt about racism in horror films. Maybe in spring semester we can plan a course on the history of Black horror films?

"Thanks for putting Dr. Coleman's *Horror Noire: Blacks in American Horror Films from the 1890s to the Present* on reserve. Her 'Introduction' blew my class away! I can hardly wait to discuss films about monsters and zombies in the hood, and end with *Get Out* and *Us*. We need a critical perspective on Black families in horror films. Couple Doc Coleman's book with Xavier Burgin's documentary based on it, and we'll blow our students' minds!

"I'm also dying to introduce the class to my Auntie's heart throb—Tony Todd of *Candyman*! Whenever that woman saw a piece of candy, she called it 'Tony' and sighed, 'It melts in your mouth.'"

Standing behind her, Tyrone shook his head, laughing and making lewd gestures with his tongue.

"A small warning on another topic, Doc. M.J. is bright and very supportive of social change. I enjoy texting her and reading her research notes. But a red flag popped up. I checked the Fairhaven graduation records and alumni news from 2018 to 2020 and 'Melody Johnson' doesn't appear in them. Do you know who else 'M.J.' stands for? Just saying. It's possible I looked for the wrong person, but I searched for undergraduates with her initials.

"I wonder what her game is? Be careful, doc! Time to go. I have less than two minutes left on this session."

Tyrone nudged her shoulder, "Oh, yeah, thanks for telling me about the relationship between Rastafarians and veganism in the U.S. Tyrone and I are considering a plant-based shift in our diets. I'm not sure we're ready to be vegans yet, but our new diet will be a good start.

"We're against unbridled white consumerism, especially of Black culture and animals. I'm delighted veganism isn't exclusively European. I also like the fact Englishman Donald Watson created the term in 1944, by squishing the word 'vegetarianism' which been around for centuries into 'veganism.' A damned clever move!"

As she signs out, Tyrone stands sideways behind her with his hands moving up and down about two feet in front of his stomach, reminding me again Aslyn is close to being a mom.

CHAPTER 9:
CADEN'S NOTES TO ASLYN
(NOVEMBER 10, 2020)

Caden read all of Ben's journal entries several times and found some trends he missed earlier. As Jackson said, "Apply Occam to see what really exists, not what you want to see."

It's hard to step outside our cultural programming, as current politics is proving, and see data and details on their own for what they are. We see everyday practices as natural, not as a social order created by powerful groups to protect their interests. We see false socially generated stories as "truth" and perpetuate them just like landowners in *The White Zombie*.

Caden once told his students, "Imagine what people see when an apple falls near the bench they're sitting on in the park. One person might see it as a snack, another as proof of gravity, and a third person as a sign from God. What's the difference? And what do you think they can agree on?"

He thought, if nothing else, Covid has highlighted our lack of critical thinking and our increased emotional states. We jump on crazy ideas like "Steal the Vote" believing them true because social media groups, our virtual communities, tell us they're true, and we want them to be true.

This morning he read social media was comparing Dr. Fauci to 16ᵗʰ century playwright Christopher Marlowe's fictional *Dr. Faustus*. It's just a matter of hours before Fauci is actually seen as Faustus—from fiction to fact. Some folks will believe he sold his soul to the devil for increased retirement income. From rumor to fact—uneffing believable, like pedophiles in pizza places. My theater colleagues must be laughing their collective asses off. This must be an awesome time for stand-up comedians on *YouTube*.

Following Aslyn's suggestion, he looked for patterns he had missed earlier. She said, "Doc, start with the Council of 5, Dr. Humphrey, and M.J."

To humor her, that night he emailed his list of observations and asked for her "Occam/Aslyn" interpretation.

The Council of 5

- Wealthy privileged white men—based on their modes of transportation (gull-wing Mercedes, helicopters, chauffeurs) and Ben's salary
- No distinguishable regional accents
- Absolute anonymity (have revealed nothing about themselves, except first names, and that's up for grabs)
- Perhaps a network of anonymous wealthy donors committed to secrecy

Dr. Humphrey

- Likes money and uses his VDP salary to prepare for retirement
- Likes older adventuresome women
- Is a well-published and respected history scholar

- Has a daughter whose mother died at her birth;
  we know only his wife's name
- Likes Southern Confederacy-based research
- Has no personal information listed anywhere, except for
  his boat, his wife's brief obit, and his professional bio,
  i.e. his academic rank, publications, college address,
  and office number (we don't even know his home address)
- Mentored Jackson and received Jackson's conference paper
  draft and tenure file on July 2, 2020 (according to his notes)
- Wears an unnerving creepy MAGA hat
- Has a strong connection with the Council because
  they mentioned changing the project timeline based
  on his recommendation

M.J.

- Unafraid to speak out about racial issues because
  she has a social conscience
- Seems in her mid-to-late 20s
- Recent WWU Fairhaven College graduate
- Has a stunning memory
- Her life, like everyone else but health care heroes and
  first responders, is on Covid pause, i.e.; will begin
  law school at UW asap
- Started work as a barista at Cafe Kaffeine in early
  September after summer graduation

He failed to mention M.J. was an eyecatcher because he didn't
want to hear Aslyn's comments.

He looked forward to her responses only to his observation list.

Aslyn has impressed him since he first met her in his evening
400-level disability in film class. A few minutes after he asked everyone to introduce themselves, Caden pointed to his syllabus projected

74

on the white board, "I have a strict absentee policy. If you miss more than four classes, you'll be docked a letter grade for each absence starting with your fifth one. We're meeting for only one three-hour session weekly, so if my class doesn't fit your schedule, consider dropping it and taking it next semester."

When he turned to write on the white board, Aslyn threw an eraser at him and missed. He picked it up, threw it back at her, hitting her on the right shoulder. The class was quiet and looked uneasy. He and Aslyn stared at each other. Then, she rose, stood at attention, and saluted him.

He asked, "Were you a Marine?" Still in a formal stance, she shouted, "Sir, yes, sir." The class remained silent as she sat down.

That was the beginning of their friendship. Two years later Caden attended her wedding, and sat with her ageing family. Tyrone later told him, "She respects you, Doc, because you didn't ignore her. She hates being told what to do, so she reacted to your absentee policy. When you threw that eraser back at her, she knew she wasn't invisible!

Grinning, Tyrone asked, "I've wondered for some time. What would you have done if a white girl had thrown that eraser at you, Doc?"

Since today is November 10, the official birthday of the Marine Corps, Caden ends his email with Happy Birthday, Marine! He almost hears Aslyn screaming "Semper Fi," but knew she wouldn't because he was just the son of a Marine, not a Marine. Maybe she and Tyrone will shout "Semper Fi!" to each other.

CHAPTER 10:
1ST F2F MEETING
(NOVEMBER 17, 2020)

Six inches of snow closed Cafe Kaffeine's outside tables, so Caden goes inside and orders a decaf mocha with hemp milk at the counter. He sits by a window and looks around for M.J., who smiles and nods at him when she comes through the kitchen doors. A few minutes later she sits down at his table, "Because of the snow, my bus route's been cancelled, and we're closing in an hour. I don't know if I can get home tonight. We need to cancel our Zoom meeting."

Caden glances at her and asks, "Where are you staying tonight?"

"Here," she says, looking at the kitchen doors.

"You can stay at my place. It's just a couple of doors down, above the paint store. I have a fold out sofa. I'll sleep there, and you can have the bedroom."

M.J. smiles, "We can have our first F2F meeting. I mean, after four Zoom meetings it'll be a good break from our routine."

"Sounds perfect. I'll wait and we can trudge through the snow together. Here's my address so you can tell your husband where you are."

She smiled, "I'm not married, or even in a relationship with anyone."

"I'm confused. I saw your wedding ring and assumed you were."

"It's not a wedding ring; it's a mourning ring. Inside it is a tiny coil of my great, great grandfather's hair. I wear it on my ring finger to keep from being hit on."

Caden thinks, "That mourning ring worked on me!" He wonders what kind of F2F meeting they'd have sitting at the same table, drinking wine, and wearing pajamas. A few hours later, he finds out.

After eating Casa's locally famous potato burritos, he starts making a quick dessert near the stove. M.J. whispers from across the table, "I don't have any sleepwear because I had no idea I couldn't get home tonight." He goes into the bedroom, pulls a thick purple bath robe from his closet, and hands it to her.

"My friend Ben gave me this on my first trip to Seattle. The hotel we stayed in had one for each guest. I liked it so much he bought it for me as a souvenir."

She excuses herself and disappears while he turns and whisks ingredients. A few minutes later, he hears a soft noise, the sound of his robe hitting the floor. He turns, and M.J. stands nude before him, her pony tail gone, and her long dark hair with red streaks cascading down over her breasts. He stares, "OMG! She's a natural blonde!" He hopes F2F meetings would replace all future Zoom meetings.

BEN'S LAST THUMB DRIVE ENTRIES
(APRIL 23, 2019 TO JULY 18, 2019)
&
CADEN'S COMMENTS

April 23, 2019: Meeting with Jackson at Sneads Ferry, N.C.

I arrived at Riverview Cafe at 5:00, knowing I'd have a few minutes before Jackson showed up. I sent him my notes and copies of Yancey Jenkins' interviews, and knew he'd be excited. At 5:15 he came in, plunked down, and put his iPad on the table, "Let's eat pie first and then dive into Occam's pool. I'm so effing hungry."

During our pie fest we watched several fishing boats cross Courthouse Bay. Jackson began, "Your Richmond notes answer many of my questions about the Verifying Data Project or the 'Validating Dead Project.' But Jenkins' interview process raises even more questions about its purpose. Why does it matter if gravesites are windy or sunny? Why do four people need to be present, and how do we get answers to the interview questions? Why are we interviewing 'discarnates'?

"Yeah, you showed us question #7 is dated, confusing, and reflects a bad product based on iffy user-testing. But, why does anyone really care? So, what does Occam's Razor tell us we don't already know, besides the questionnaire is a product of bad user design? Why focus on each grave's atmosphere?"

I watched shrimp boats and an occasional MCAS helicopter and prepared myself for a Jackson rant. He leaned back, opened his iPad, and smiled, "Let's look at new info. You knew CPA means Confederate Psychic Association, but you probably didn't know MAGA means 'Mediums Against Government Action,' an organization Yancey founded. Didn't see that one coming, huh?

"Hell, no!" I shook my head with my mouth open.

He continued, "It's obvious the Council of 5 is trolling for info from a constituency they trust: dead Confederate soldiers and their dead white male descendants buried slightly before and during the Jim Crow era. MAGAites will use their collective psychic powers to restrict and suppress government actions stepping on their 'freedoms.' Ironically, Jamie thinks the VDP is really the 'Voting Dead Project,' a clever disguise for idiots to protect their freedom and create the old country they nostalgically dream of!

"Even bigger voting questions arise. How do mediums interview discarnates, register them, and get their votes counted for future Presidential elections?"

I was just getting ready to answer when a tall, well-built smiling Black man dressed in workout togs walked in. He nodded to a group of smiling older women wearing tennis shoes sitting at a table near the bay window. They stared at his FUBU hustle shorts and rippling tight tee shirt as he moved in our direction. He reminded me of a young Carl Lewis, or a model in the *Men's Journal*. I noticed the women lean into one another and whisper; some even glowed as he passed them.

He stopped, stood behind Jackson, put his left hand on Jackson's shoulder, and squeezed. Without looking up, Jackson smiled, "Ben, I want you to meet Jamie, my partner."

Jamie said, "Husband," as he pulled up a seat and waved to our server, a well-built, fit woman probably in her late 40s. He grinned at me, "Every woman here is in one or more of my fitness classes."

I'd never seen Jackson smile as much or look happier, except when he mentioned Jamie. I had missed a few Occam moments in past conversations.

Jamie sat down, and Jackson squeezed his hand, "I asked Jamie to join us and go over your notes. Even though he isn't one, he comes from a long line of Louisiana psychics, so I thought maybe he could shed light on your notes and be the edge of our sharp, stunning Occam's Razor."

Our server brought Jamie a vegan meal, so I knew my Carl Lewis observation was a good one. After dinner, Jackson and I summarized what we pulled from our notes, and I asked for Jamie's thoughts.

Drinking seltzer water mixed with mango juice, Jamie offered these insights based on what Jackson told him while he worked at Oakdale:

1) The attention on grave environments tells us Yancey worries about cell phone reception
2) The Council believes the life/death binary doesn't exist
3) The word 'disabled' tells us the CPA and MAGA consider death an impairment
4) The Council wants graves to become polling places
5) The Council considers white discarnates victims of voter suppression
6) The project focuses on voting rights for dead white men
7) As sponsors of this project, the Council probably plans to extend the Voting Rights Act only to "discarnate" Confederates and their "discarnate" offspring.

"I believe you all owe me a glass of exceptional wine for this answer."

He grinned at Jackson, and they slapped palms.

I had an Occam moment! "Jesus, the Council has brought together psychics, voting, disability lawyers, and the Lost Cause— all to please both MAGAs. What the hell does this mean, and where is it going?"

Jackson, who almost forgot I was at the table, turned away from me, and rolled his eyes at Jamie, "They'll use the ADA signed by President Bush and its 2008 update to accommodate the voting dead. Question #7 implies 'death' is a 'disability.' By linking death, disability, and voting sites, the Council is rehearsing a new voting process to verify burial sites as voting sites!"

I blurted out, "This new voting process builds on the rising social media campaign on voter suppression! Conservative news commentators, MAGAites, and social media groups rallying their followers, will shake their fists, and scream, 'White Dead Men Matter!' The VDP is a way of voter rigging to guarantee predictable future votes from an ignored dead demographic. Dammit, the VDP redefines voter fraud and 'Steal the Vote.'"

Jackson lowered his voice, "In a perverse way, this project is chill. Many politicians support voter suppression to protect their parties by complicating the voting process to eliminate populations who don't look or think like them, just another way of rigging an election. Others make voting easier for everyone, especially the BIPOC demographic, college students, veterans, the working class, rural residents, the poor, the elderly, and people with disabilities. The VD Project appeals to both viewpoints and blurs binary thinking. Allowing the dead to vote removes one type of voter discrimination but replaces it with another by privileging dead white male voters over all other discarnates. Graveside voting redefines 'voter suppression.' Talk about kicking binary thinking in the butt! Makes you rethink gerrymandering, intersectionality, and redistricting! Gives new meaning to cattywampus!"

Jamie shook his head, laughed, and spewed mango seltzer water across Jackson's iPad, "It's funny, but sadly possible, given these times."

I wondered if the VD Project will be the next giant step away from democracy.

Caden's Comments

What was Ben thinking when he wrote these entries? He still doesn't see where this pattern is leading them. 'Voter Suppression' and the 'Voting Dead Project' are stretches of the imagination. Maybe the three of them are just seeing what they want to see.

Jamie's witty and very funny! He's not the partner I thought Jamie would be…my bad. I missed the pattern and assumed he was a blonde cheerleader. He's the perfect match for Jackson, and his observations are amazing.

The VD Project is getting creepier than Hamlet's mother. Ben wrote this entry on Shakespeare's birthday, so "Happy late Birthday, Will!" I wonder what Shakespeare would write in this political climate.

April 24, 2019: Dr. Humphrey on My New Interview Questions

Oakdale Cemetery is a florist's dream in the spring and reminds me of Hollywood Cemetery. The scents and colors calmed me. I met Dr. Humphrey, Yancey, and the interns at the Confederate Mound. We looked like tourists taking a slow walking tour of Oakdale; we were as invisible as Black senior citizens as we took photos, posed together, and dictated notes into our cell phones.

Dr. Humphrey stopped by for an update of our work. He was on his way to visit Georgia cemeteries near Stone Mountain Park, the Southern version of Mount Rushmore, one of the most visited tourist attractions in Georgia.

We all left the Mound and headed for ten graves to beta test our new focused questionnaire. I reduced the original interview template to four questions:

1) Do you believe you are dead?
2) Do your miss your body?
3) Do you have sons?
4) Have you ever voted?

Impressed, Humphrey said, "These questions help us ignore discarnates who are too dumb or too wasted to vote. If they pass this test, they 'qualify' for our revised 9-question survey."

The new interns smiled and nodded their heads.

Over the next few hours we interviewed ten discarnates with Yancey and learned four of them couldn't hear us at all, and the other 6 answered "Yes" to each question. I wondered if this sample reflects the number of discarnates who can't or won't cast ballots. I don't think it ever occurred to the Council that not all dead Southerners supported or believed in the Lost Cause.

Some Southerners saw the Lost Cause as a contrived "false consciousness," and rejected the wealthy culture's whitewashed perspective on slavery as "natural." I read in the National Archives that somewhere around 45 Southerners received Medals of Honor during the Civil War, an honor given only to U.S. soldiers. After the Emancipation Act in 1862, 10% of the Union soldiers were Black and 15 of them received Medals of Honor.

If Dr. Humphrey's right, we'll expand our time frame to make up for those discarnates who didn't vote or won't cast future ballots, even if they didn't leave the South. In a bizarre way, the VD Project is making sense.

Caden's Comments

Crap, I see Ben's point about whitewashing. Why do most people assume all Southerners who supported the Lost Cause stayed in the South? After the war, some Confederates were fed up with the new America they saw and fled. About 20,000 Confederados filled with resentment and anger left the country after the Civil War. They emigrated to San Paola, Brazil, eventually created the city 'Americana,' embraced their new independence, and modified their beliefs over time. In 1972, five years before becoming President, Georgia Governor Jimmy Carter visited them.

Just another forgotten moment that clashes with Humphrey and Yancey's concept of Southern history.

April 29, 2019: Martha's Vineyard 2ⁿᵈ Visit

I arrived on a Monday this time. The Black Dog Tavern was open, and I actually ate food, not airplane snacks. I gorged on Loaded Quinoa and walked uphill. Smiling as I passed the graveyard near my cabin, I stopped, stared at the stars, breathed deeply, and grinned because I make so much money. I ordered a vegan hummus tray with pita and paid to have it delivered to my cabin.

The next day, I met the Council of 5 midmorning in the community room at the Universal Church in Vineyard Haven, not far from my cabin. Even though I only had met them once, I immediately recognized them. They all had name cards in front of themselves—James, Thomas, Lawrence, William, and Jonathan.

Thomas spoke, "We thank you for your comments on Yancey Jenkin's questionnaire, and for demonstrating how necessary user-testing is for our project. On Dr. Humphrey's advice, we've moved the time frame back to 1835. These 21 extra years will offset the 40% loss we anticipate from discarnates who can't or won't participate in the study. We didn't realize some discarnates don't want to repeat the past. Thank you for showing us the problem." He twisted his wedding ring and rubbed his palm with his thumb.

James spoke: "We want to update you on our project. As you know, the Verifying Data process is only phase 1 and 2 in our long range 'The Voting Dead Project.'

Thomas handed out a one-page overview of Phase 3 and 4 of The Voting Dead Project timeline. "In the next few months, we want you to initiate 'Phase 3,' our marketing plan.

Phase 3: Marketing Plan (Ongoing)
- Observe trends in fake news and conspiracy theories
- Legally redefine death
- Initiate legal changes which link cemeteries
  and disability laws

"We'll meet in Seattle in 90 days, on July 27. Look over your data, and prepare for Phase 4: The 8-year Project Implementation (2020-2028)."

I left the Vineyard shaking my head, "Jamie nailed it again! Who's really behind the Voting Dead Project? What are their goals?

How did they know we figured VDP might be the 'Voting Dead Project?'"

May 1, 2019: Surf City, N.C.

I pulled into the parking lot of the posh six-story condo, set back from the surf, overlooking the beach. Jackson and Jamie live on the top floor. Jamie's gym and fitness club "Fit 4 Tomorrow" occupies the ground floor.

I parked the Range Rover at a space near the edge of a sand dune where Jamie and Jackson had arranged for AmeriCorps interns to plant rows of native plants to stop storm erosion. I recognized sea oats and St. John's wort, LJB's favorite plants, growing on the dune nearest me. It was probably just one of a number of community service projects Jackson and Jamie contributed to. It must cost a small fortune to sponsor such projects. When I turn 50, I'll bet LJB's skinny ass he'll expect me to donate to the community around my Oregon beach house.

I walked through the large open lobby to the elevator and realized they are "the" 6th floor. On my 50th birthday I can buy an entire floor, not just a room on a floor. Smirking, I stepped inside the elevator. A minute later, the elevator door opened inside a huge living room with an incredible view of sand dunes, the beach, and ocean waves. Jackson was standing in front of the sofa where Jamie sat. With his back to the floor to ceiling window, I heard him singing *Sixteen Tons*, reminding me of my late grandparents' annual Labor Day party. My Granddad always smiled when he sang the chorus about "the company store" as he swilled martinis. Jackson finished the song, bowed, and smiled at Jamie.

Jackson looked at me and said, "*Sixteen Tons* written in 1946 and made famous in 1955 resonates with today's ignored work force, too, especially people of color, women, and poor people in general. It wasn't their blood but their souls corporations owned. Damn shame they didn't have social media as we know it."

Jamie stood, applauded, smiled, noticed me, and said, "My man can think and sing, too."

Stopping halfway across the room, I asked, "Remember *The Texas Chainsaw Massacre?*"

They looked at me with heads turned sideways… "Yeah?"

"Jackson's right! In 1975, Tobe Hooper's cannibalistic butcher family eats their murder victims who stop at their gas station, offering a personal solution to high gas prices and supply chain demand after the Arab oil embargo. Hooper's critique shows society victimizing workers and everyday people, something that hasn't changed in almost 50 years."

For the first time, they both slapped my hands. I knew Caden would have smiled because I saw *TCM* with him in Richmond.

We ate dinner on the balcony. The sun set behind us, exactly the opposite direction of my new place in Point Roberts, surrounded by the Salish Sea and views of the Canadian Rockies, San Juan Islands, and Washington's Mount Baker. I watched seagulls dip into the ebbing tide looking for small crabs. I realized how much I missed the curling bark of Madrona trees and the rustle of birch leaves in the Pacific Northwest wind. Hell, I even longed to see cottonwood fluff partially covering sidewalks and roads!

I told them of my meeting with the Council and its focus on marketing in Phase 3, especially on observing social media and fake news trends as well as linking cemeteries to disability laws. Jackson perked up and waved a mosquito off his face, "We feel an Occam moment coming! Jamie, want to go first?"

Jamie smiled, "Here's my take on social media and how it might relate to VDP. Remember Trump's supporters bragging about his IQ and how social media raved about his IQ being among the highest of all U.S. Presidents?"

We nodded.

"How did dead Presidents take the test?"

Jamie's theory on the social media's blathering on about the President's IQ oddly fits the VDP. Laughing hard, he explained:

"The IQ test most of us know is the Stanford-Binet Test, the 1905 French test revised and released in 1916 by a researcher from Stanford University. Many people, teachers, and union leaders, not politicians, felt the test was biased in favor of the privileged. They saw it as a plan against immigrants and the poor, a hurdle to their education and employment, just another way to keep the working class invisible and working.

"So, how can we know the IQs of the 27 Presidents serving before 1916? And how can we compare those born after 1916 with any President if they never took an IQ test? Kind of makes you wonder about our social media's IQ."

I remembered the Cornell decades-long Stupid Study by Dr. David Dunning, and wondered if the IQ diversion is an example of "Stupidity Squared."

In a study last year, researchers on the Dunning-Kruger Effect discovered even if we don't know much about the topic, we overestimate our knowledge in certain areas and become even more confident if our social environment is one we really like or want to belong to. A political candidate who wants to impress their party or their followers will project self-confidence and a sense of knowledge about a topic, say climate change or immigration, even though they really know little about it. Their followers buy into it. And the media jumps on it. A real shit show.

Jackson flicked another mosquito off his nose and took over, "Important people have critiqued the pursuit of money for more than 500 years. World leaders and intellectuals saw uncontrolled wealth as a dominant Western theme, from Sir Thomas More's 'conspiracy of the rich,' Camus' 1946 'Human Crisis' speech at Columbia University,

Eisenhower's 'grave implications of the military-industrial complex,' to Dr. King's evils of capitalism.

"But our favorite critique is Pope Frances' recent allusion to 14th century St. Basil of Caesarea, who called unbridled capitalism the 'dung of the devil' and the cause of the Western mistreatment of American indigenous people." They bumped wine glasses.

Without thinking, I blurted, "Holy shit."

Jamie nodded, "No ... the opposite! These folks all slam financial conspiracies which place money over humanity. It's easy to see how the rich embrace money, ignore workers, people of color, indigenous people. They manipulate self-centered politicians who place party over people to protect their assets or in most cases their asses.

"Historically, many wealthy folks swayed voting to prevent childcare for workers, free education, health care for everyone, and a universal basic monthly income to reduce homelessness and poverty. Don't even get me started on reparations for systemic racist treatment of Black and indigenous people. The solution for me is simple: What would Jesus do?"

Jamie eased back into his chair, poured himself another glass of wine, "I now pass the microphone to you, my dear Jackson."

He nodded and looked at me, "We have Jenkins's data from his interviews. According to him, question #7 was a snafu. The discarnates got confused over 'disabled,' and you rushed in and saved the day. Here's my Occam moment: The Council will link 'dead' and 'disabled.' I'll bet Humphrey's fat saggy ass the Council will define death as a disability; you know, a missing body is like a missing limb, an impairment requiring accommodations in public spaces.

Jackson raised his glass and said, "The 2008 Americans with Disability Amendment Act requires access for all to public spaces, which cemeteries oddly are. Unfortunately, the ADA uses the word 'accommodation' which implies doing someone a favor rather than treating them as equals. Two steps forward, one step backwards.

"In a way, an accommodation is a compromise, an act offering another option to binary thinkers. An accommodation critiques binary thinking which sees people only with and without impairments and says, 'Let's create an environment everyone can use'—a progressive move!"

Jamie glanced at Jackson and smiled.

Jackson continued, "So graves in cemeteries are public spaces requiring accessibility accommodations. If 'disabled' and 'dead' become legally synonymous, then cemeteries can become voting places for discarnates. Since discarnates lack bodies, some kind of accommodation, say mediums with cell phones, must be available for them to vote! Because we haven't yet accommodated them, they must be supported by the 2008 ADA Amendment Act!"

I thought, "He sounds like Caden on one of his disability rolls." I sipped my wine, looked out over the incoming surf and white cumulus clouds on the horizon and blurted, "Shit!" and quickly apologized.

They looked at each other and shook their heads. Jamie said, "Back to you, my dear Jackson."

Jackson nodded, "Jamie made some good points, but something else occurs to me. Geez, it's right in front of us. The Council's reliance on Southern mediums got me thinking. If Jenkins is the head of the CPA, and not an academic, how did he connect with Dr. Humphrey, who's a smart academic, but money focused, and even good to me?

"I mean, are Council members wealthy mediums rejecting change or just a white privileged group chasing big bucks? If we break the binary, they can be both, the original MAGA supporters and Mediums Against Government Action, who want to resurrect the past to increase their power and wealth. Either way, how far will the Council go to make its dreams come true? No one has ever met them, besides you. No one working on the VDP has met them; even Dr. Humphrey said he's never met them."

A bright light flashed across my mind, and I shouted, "It's not a Council, it's a Cabal! Yes, I've met them…sat in the same room with them twice. They seem like wealthy white guys with no discernible accents. I'm sure Humphrey's met them, too. He contacted them after our last meeting in Wilmington to let them know about my changing Yancey's interview questions. And they relied on Humphrey to expand their time frame. That's all I can tell you. I'm worried we know too much."

We sat in silence as Jackson made a list of takeaways all pointing to a wealthy corporate Cabal working underground with some members of our government. I continued, "They believe changing voting laws is the only way to preserve the past to protect their finances and guarantee future income. I see Eisenhower's military-industrial complex rising on the horizon and democracy as we know it slipping over the edge."

Slapping another mosquito, Jackson's final questions were: "How far will they go? And who are their supporters and partners?"

Looking sad, Jamie leaned into Jackson and muttered, "POP! POP!"

Confused, I asked, "What the hell is a 'POP, POP'?"

Jackson turned towards me, "Party Over People."

On my way out as the elevator closed, I heard Jackson singing to Jamie, "Black is the color…." He's no Rhiannon Giddens, but he's damn good.

May 4, 2019: Oakdale Cemetery Interview Results

Before returning home, I spent three days in Wilmington meeting with Dr. Humphrey's new interns, looking over their notes, and texting Yancey in Richmond about emerging trends. Using my revised questionnaire, his interns visited more than half of Hollywood's selected graves three times, and only 10% of their discarnates got confused or didn't answer the questions, a 30% decrease in discarnate confusion over earlier interviews. Substituting "dead" for "disabled" in Question #7 worked! In his last text message, Yancey's grinning avatar told me, "Because of your revised questionnaire, my Hollywood interns' findings exceeded those of the Oakdale group."

I was pleased because I saw a small raise on the horizon, "Hell, yes!"

July 2, 2019: Jackson's Tenure File Request

Hey, Ben,

A quick ask for help? You mentioned you commented on Caden's file when he went up for tenure at VCU. Jamie suggested I run my tenure file by you for advice. He thinks I should get advice from someone other than Dr. Ahh (Ass-Hole Humphrey) as Jamie now calls him. Please think about it.

I feel my file is good, but I'm too close to it, and I need your user-testing expertise. I have solid student evaluations, 5 publications in refereed journals, solid community service, excluding volunteering with Dr. Humphrey and his interns. I've also presented 7 papers at national conferences during my 4 years at Wilmington City College. I think I fit well within the academic hierarchy.

Here's the abstract of the paper I'm sending off to the American Historical Association (AHA) for presentation at their annual convention in New Orleans in January. If they accept it, it'll show how current and significant my research is. I'm dropping it off to Humphrey tomorrow. Since he's my department head and a well-known scholar, his advice and letter of support will almost guarantee the college granting me tenure.

Jamie said, "Don't count on it from Dr. Ahh." He's really bothered by the fact Humphrey kept his links to the Cabal secret from me. But I'm sure he wants me to succeed to make his transition into retirement easy.

ABSTRACT *"Changing Binary Paradigms and Their Impact in a Politically Divisive Society"*

By carefully rethinking long held binary beliefs such as abled/disabled and living/dead, one covert manipulative group will create a tomorrow based on our whitewashed past. This paper discusses one example of change that on the surface could help everyone, but in reality, helps only secretive powermongers who will resurrect the past to protect their investments as they value politics over people.

This paper describes how the nefarious "Voting Dead Project" rejects the living/dead binary, offering in its place a new model of discarnate consciousness defining death from a different perspective, not just on the brain/body or the conscious/unconscious binary. This clandestine project run by an unknown capitalist Cabal manipulates Diversity, Equity, and Inclusion (DEI) and creates a new kind of voter suppression which relies on unbridled social media.

As we redefine death and connect it to disability, we'll see voting laws change to accommodate all voters. But in the near future, this new voter suppression model will rise, allowing only selected dead white males to vote. This new model will replace redistricting, vote rigging, and voter suppression as we know it. The Cabal is quietly working hard to create a white male demographic to restore Jim Crow laws and overturn voting progress since the Civil Rights Act. Until EVERY dead person can vote, not just white males, our problematic past will rise again.

It'd be awesome if I could have your revision suggestions by the end of the month, so I can meet AHA's August deadline. Thanks, brother!

Jamie sends a big, brotherly hug.

Jackson, soon to be a tenured Associate Professor!

PS. As usual, Jamie applied Occam and saw that "vote," "voters," and "voting" appear more than 50 times in Humphrey and Yancey's VDP documents. How the hell did we miss that pattern?

PPS. Soon after I earn tenure and promotion, I plan to launch my new podcast, "The Voting Dead Project Exposed." Yep, it really is the Voting Dead Project, not the Verifying Data Project! I'll send you my link early next year when my podcast is up and running.

July 6, 2019: Unexpected News

"Ben, let's meet soon. I can't talk now. My world and my heart exploded!"

Attached to his email is today's news from the *Wilmington Star*:

"Jamie Lazarus Nealy (April 23, 1990 - July 5, 2019), victim of a hit and run accident by an unidentified vehicle, died during his daily 5-mile sunrise run at Topsail Beach, N.C.

Jamie was born in New Orleans, Louisiana, where he helped his family run a large community garden in his parish. His mother, grand-mother, and aunt were gifted psychics and descendants of Marie Laveau, the famous 19th century Voodoo queen of the Creole community. He leaves behind his husband Jackson Canaday. Nealy graduated from Appalachian State University, Boone, N.C., in 2012.

His love for long distance running led him to a successful fitness career. He was the founder and owner of Fit 4 Tomorrow Centers, a chain of East coast fitness centers headquartered in Surf City on Topsail Island, N.C. He was often quoted in the media, 'Exercise gives us time to think and connect with our past, present, and future.'

A memorial service will be held in the Fit 4 Tomorrow Center on the ground floor of the Surf City Condominiums on August 1, 2019. A buffet with non-alcoholic drinks and vegan foods will be available for those celebrating his life. Instead of flowers, please send donations to the Topsail Island Food Bank or the Southern Poverty Law Center."

July 7, 2019: Leaving Point Roberts, WA

I closed my iPad and stared across the water at White Rock, B.C. Usually high tide, boats, and the Canadian Rockies make me smile, but today I sat silently on my deck. I couldn't imagine Jackson's pain. In the clouds above the B.C. mountains, I saw Jamie's grin, not my asshole dad's grimace.

I'll help Jackson grieve and put his tenure file together. It's the least I can do. After all, I do most of my data sorting on my computer, so I don't need to be back here until July 27, when I'm meeting the Cabal in Seattle. I'll help Jackson commemorate Jamie, his reason for living.

My goal is focused on Phase 3 Marketing Plan (TBA). I've been spending too much time watching Fox News, following FB, Twitter, Instagram, TikTok, listening to podcasts, skimming the Twitter King's tweets, and following hilarious new politically charged social media trends. I'm studying the American Disability Act (1990) and its 2008 amendment, which gives people with disabilities more clout in the legal system rather than just acknowledging and then legally writing them off as the ADA often did. Fascinating stuff and not as boring as conspiracy theories and blame games. I could use Caden's disability expertise now.

A cross-country flight might help me think. Yancey knows the disability angle well, and in his last email he sent me several links to legal websites. After touching base with Jackson, I'll meet Yancey in Wilmington, go over his interview stats, and look for new trends.

I dropped by my condo's business office to ask Melanie Jensen, our new HOA associate manager, to gather my mail and water my plants while I'm gone. She helped me earlier in March, when I drove to Vancouver, B.C., to splurge on Canadian vegan fare and wine because I needed three BAD days (Ben Alone Days) and short walks through Stanley Park to see Occam patterns. With her blonde hair, Melanie looks like the blonde autistic young woman in *Please Stand By*, the last movie I saw with Caden for his "Disability in Film" class for VCU. She's attractive, smart, wears incredible jewelry (a different antique ring daily), loves to hold hands while walking and sleeping, looks unbelievable in the nude, and has an incredible memory.

Her Tidewater accent charmed the hell out of me and reminded me of several young women I met at Virginia Beach during my brief tour at the Norfolk Naval Air Station. I'm sure whatever I ask her to do will get done, and she'll anticipate problems before they arise.

July 8, 2019: Jackson's Last Email

"Been there, done that…Ben Dunn!" Don't know why Jamie and I didn't see it coming. We turned our backs on Occam and Jamie paid for it!

The pattern was right in front of us. You told the Council I was blowing up their project, described my tenure file, told them about my AHA conference paper, and my plans to launch my Voting Dead podcast and blog. Discarnate Jamie will come after you. Don't think about getting in touch with me! You despicable soulless bastard!

July 8, 2019: My Quick Visit to Surf City

Words escaped me. I texted Jackson, "I did NOT tell anyone about your work. I'm leaving soon for Wilmington. Let's meet in Sneads Ferry at 5:00 on the 10th and sort this out. I'm worried someone's hacking our email and snail mail. I'll call as soon as I land. I'm sorry for your losing Jamie, an incredible person. My heart's broken, too. Let's grieve and celebrate him together. Please, please, please, be fucking careful!"

Near midnight on the 9th, I arrived in foggy, humid Wilmington, called Jackson, left a message, and rented a car. I'm staying in an upscale resort at Carolina Beach, a few miles from Oakdale Cemetery. Tomorrow, I'll drop in on him and explain I haven't told anyone about his tenure file or his other publicity plans. I was wary of the Cabal and now A.H. Humphrey, who's the only other person to see Jackson's tenure file.

I'll meet Jackson in Sneads Ferry and ask how I can help with Jamie's memorial service. Together, we'll praise Jamie, and reflect on his insights. I wondered why Jackson thought Jamie's death was murder and not an accidental hit and run?

During the flight to Wilmington, I'll study the interns' data. More importantly, I need to hear Yancey's views, so I can clearly connect "death, disability, mediums, graves, and voting" to figure out the direction the Council is moving.

I read an article on perceptions of dying and learned we define death in several different ways: legal, medical, ethical/moral, and spiritual. New paradigms challenged our cultural perspectives. In France, you could marry your dead partner to receive their estate. In England some medical and legal communities defined death by shifting focus from lack of heartbeat to lack of brainstem function. Even if the heart still beat, if the brain was nonfunctioning, the person was legally and medically dead.

Damn, I finally got it: we need to define where consciousness exists. Is consciousness in the physical or spiritual world? Or as a nonbinary thinker would say, "In both!" I needed a day with Yancey and to read more about neuroplasticity, the rewiring of the brain, and its relationship to phantom limbs and death.

On my way to the Riverside Cafe in Sneads Ferry, I drove to Topsail Island and pulled into the Fit 4 Tomorrow Center parking lot. A large poster of handsome smiling Jamie graced the front window. A smaller poster announced the details of the August 1 Memorial Celebration and described Jamie's favorite exercises for calmness, thinking, and inner peace. I opened the door, saw another poster of Jamie with older women surrounding him. I smiled, bowed my head, and walked in. I touched Jamie's face on the poster, glanced at the reception room, and saw no one. I returned to my car, and drove to Sneads Ferry.

Jackson never responded to my texts or my call expressing my sorrow about Jamie. I hoped he'd be at the cafe, sitting by the window watching helicopters cross Court House Bay. I wanted to talk, grieve, fist bump, and slap hands with him.

I didn't see Jackson when I arrived at 5:00. I waited for 30 minutes, swirled sweet ice tea, and then ordered dinner, just hush puppies and coleslaw to keep me focused until I can buy a real fresh seafood dinner for him. By 7:30 I knew he wasn't coming. I paid my bill and drove back to Topsail Island. As I passed Jackson's condo, I slowed down and noticed the blinds were drawn and lights were out on the 6th floor.

I shook my head and wiped my eyes with my shirt sleeve.

July 11, 2019: Meeting Yancey at Carolina Beach

I arrived early at the small restaurant near my hotel on Carolina Beach. Wearing his MAGA cap, Yancey came in at 9:00 a.m., dropped off his laptop, a book bag, and a folded issue of today's *Wilmington Star-News*. He excused himself, and headed for the bathroom, mumbling, "I'll be awhile. Order a decaf coffee for me, and feel free to read my paper."

His wallet fell out of his book bag. As I picked it up, I saw a photo of a smiling young woman with her arms wrapped around him. Judging from her black robe, the photo was shot at her college graduation. Her hair was dark brown with red highlights. She looked like she could be Melanie's sister. Her uncanny resemblance made me smile and think how lucky Yancey was. I slipped the wallet back into the book bag and opened the paper.

After scanning the big national stories, I turned to local news. Filling one column of the first page of the "Local" section is this blurb:

"*Dr. Jackson Canaday's body was found late last night on North Topsail Island. Flounder giggers found him in the mud flats just yards from where his husband was killed last week in a hit and run accident....*"

I opened my mouth and stared at the article. The room shrunk and blurred for a minute or two.

When he returned, Yancey asked, "Are you OK?"

I pointed at the article. He stared at it and shook his head, "I didn't know Jackson was married to a Black man."

I sat still, my mouth slightly ajar. I get what my D.I. always told us, "There are more dickheads in the world than dicks."

Yancey continued, "Jackson was a good man. I wonder if he committed suicide in his depression and sorrow over losing Jamie?"

As he spoke, I realized Jackson wouldn't kill himself before memorializing Jamie, his true love and best friend. How did Yancey know Jamie's name? WTF! What would Occam see, here? I want to scream at the surf, drag Yancey face down across the sand, and smash his head with a beach rock. I'd like to tattoo "Dick" across his forehead. But I sat still and quiet.

Yancey began, "I have only two hours before catching the Richmond air shuttle." He opened his computer, "I liked Jackson. He was a smart guy and supervised our interns better than any MAGAite. We'll really miss him."

I bit my lip and nodded.

Yancey pulled out my list of questions about disability voting accommodations and handed me a 3-page typed response with a reference list. As he rambled on, all I thought of were Jackson's last words to me, "You soulless bastard."

Yancey looked around, glanced at his watch, and talked faster, "Many psychics and parapsychologists believe death is just life continuing on a new level. Organizations such as the Confederate Psychics Association, the University of Virginia's Division of Perceptual

Studies (UDOPS), and the University of Arizona's groundbreaking work on its soon to be released SoulPhone, all question our perception of death. These thoughts aren't just academic thoughts; they're nearly 4,900 paranormal societies in the U.S. with more than half of them in the South who question death as we've known it.

"You can see why our bosses are pushing so hard to get our voting model in play before social media spreads our plans across the states to other groups, especially women, indigenous people, people of color, and LGBTQs. Once our work hits the internet, we're screwed because other demographics will imitate our model and use grave-yards as voting booths. Imagine what will happen if BIPOC folks, women, and people under 30 organize discarnate voting campaigns! Their numbers will skew future elections and create unwanted new future paths for America!"

I sipped coffee and bit into a Krispy Krème doughnut, knowing I could eat a dozen before he wound down.

"Our discretion and secrecy will make sure discarnate white Southern men vote first before all other dead voters. When we succeed, the glorious true past of the Lost Cause will be resurrected because we'll create laws to prevent future socialist changes. We must move fast to beat other groups from researching cemeteries and grave-yards and getting their demographics to vote."

I can't believe what I'm hearing. Jamie was correct as usual. He figured out the VD Project really is the "Voting Dead Project" several days before the Council told me. How the hell did I ignore the data patterns for so long?

Yancey stared at his MAGA cap, and his eyes teared up, "This is why Mediums Against Government Action exists: to make sure all dead white males who have been systemically ignored, mistreated, and abused as suppressed voters have the right to vote first."

He leaned forward, his voice cracking, "In the 2016 election, with the exception of Virginia and its Democratic governor, all 12

Southern states voted for Trump. Manipulate the original MAGA supporters, Republican governors and their followers, paranormal societies, cemeteries with Confederate dead, and you have a new robust voting block that guarantees future election outcomes in perpetuity for corporations and white people fearing change."

I excused myself, walked to the sidebar, filled my coffee cup, and brought back two Krispy Kremes, which I placed on my paper napkin.

Yancey droned on, "The Council chose Virginia and North Carolina with their past Jim Crow practices as test sites for the voting dead. Nearly one quarter of the Confederate dead are buried in these two states. If the Council succeeds, more than two hundred thousand new discarnate voters from these states alone will vote in the next few Presidential elections. This new voting block will influence enough votes to elect the politicians the Council wants.

"Originally, we expected more than one million voters, but many discarnates don't want to participate and many of them answered 'No,' telling us they want changes from their former lives. Even so, this new voter demographic of staunch Lost Cause supporters will swing elections in several states, keeping red states red, and returning us to the glorious past before the War of Northern Aggression. Just imagine the election results if all Confederate states use the new voting procedures we're creating!"

"The War of Northern Aggression!" I kept my mouth shut, chewed on my cheek, and raised my eyebrows as he nodded, smiled, and grabbed his book bag. Yancey put on his new MAGA cap and left quietly for the airport.

A couple of hours later, I sat on the beach with a six pack from the Food Lion and ate a collard greens veggie wrap. I needed comfort food to read Yancey's notes. His soliloquy before leaving was a summary of page one. Pages two and three were as oddly chilling as page one, but focused on Disability Law and the 1993 National Voting

Rights Act, also called the "Motor Voter Law," which expanded voter registration opportunities.

Yancey saw Section 7 of the NVRA as the pivot point for the real future. He planned to redefine cemeteries as external sites for local and state voter registration offices. He felt gravesite voter registration complied as "specialized assistance" opportunities for discarnates, people with disabilities.

Wiping vinegar and hot sauce off my fingers in the sand, I wondered if social media and its followers would ever look at voter fraud the same way again, if and when the dead can register and vote. Face it, none of these discarnate voters, not one of them, had ever experienced the internet and social media. For the Council to succeed, they must review their cemetery interview survey data and ignore the small discarnate demographic who will vote for social change. I turned pages and jotted down my notes.

Yancey had written, "The easiest solution is secrecy. Convince state politicians yearning for the 'good ol' days' to hide their VDP changes in other laws and keep them from the public through social media diversion for at least two consecutive Presidential elections. As the U.S. political blame game continues and the Council misdirects public attention, I'm sure we can change the future by relying on the past and allowing only those to vote who answered 'Yes' on question #8: 'Do you wish to preserve the America you or your ancestors fought for?'"

I put his notes down, popped open another beer, and continued reading. I smiled because Yancey's tone sounded like Caden's tenure file overview before I made editorial suggestions.

"Our religious beliefs often reject legal and medical views of life and death. Many religions see a timed space between life and death, like bardo and purgatory. Most of us feel life continues in some form after physical death. The Council wants voters to assume death is just one phase in an ongoing existence. When the body goes, the spirit stays. For them, the spirit and consciousness are inseparable, a win for us!"

Yeah…yeah…binaries…I get it. Jesus. I pulled the tab on another beer.

"The body is a temporary container housing a living soul. Losing a body is no different than losing an arm. Phantom limb and phantom pain, long-known in the medical world, reflect conscious existence of a body part after it is severed. If the limb is gone, why and how does the person still feel its movement? Even our bodies challenge our binary concept of life/death and make us consider what else we're missing?

"My point is this: if death is a spirit minus the body, we must accommodate the spirit to acknowledge its current state. The Council wants like-minded politicians to accept dead white Southern men as systemically suppressed voters, a crime against the dead when their votes are ignored and abused by living people. We must provide an equivalent to the 24-hour voting drop box for discarnates, citizens with disabilities, who cannot leave their graves to vote. Voter suppression as we know it will end once we introduce our plan to social media. We must move quickly before other groups register their dead."

His explanation of blurred binaries straddles logic and irrationality, a good fit for social media. I saw why the Cabal hired him.

"Thanks in large part to my interpretation of section III of the 2008 ADAA, we'll legally define death as a permanent 'impairment.' When we do so, we'll have no problem convincing our like-minded politicians and voters to treat graves as voting booths, and cell phones, like SoulPhones, as accommodations.

"Many people think change pushes us into the future where we really can't be sure of anything. Think about it, if we're always changing, we're always getting too many ideas, and we'll soon be like animal hoarders, but it's our brains and not our houses that'll be full of crap.

"Our interns in Oakdale Cemetery found none of the discarnates in their survey have changed their beliefs since dying. In fact, one man who died in 1947 has not changed his views on anything since then. Imagine 72 years of consistency! This makes him a perfect voter who wants to restore his political world and make his America great again.

"Isn't it our right to hold onto our beliefs in spite of how much new information we've been exposed to? In this free country shouldn't we at 45 be able to believe the same things we did at 18? The VDP is the best solution to an unpredictable changing world!"

Unnerved, I sat still, put his notes down, and remembered Yancey holding back tears as he left for the airport. For the first time, I noticed his wedding ring looked similar to Melanie's mourning ring which contained hair from her great, great grandfather, a Confederate General. When I looked out the window, I imagined Occam's sad face as he shook his head in the clouds.

July 16, 2019: My Return to Point Roberts

Sometimes I forget how beautiful the coast of Washington is, especially the Point. Being gone for a week reminded me of what I'd missed when I returned. I dropped by the condo office and retrieved my key and snail mail from Melanie, whom I thanked profusely, and asked if she'd like to come over for dinner this evening, and I thought, "Maybe a hand holding session."

I realized someone, probably Melanie, straightened up my desk because I left a mess in my rush to get to Wilmington. My thumb drive containing emails to Caden, Jackson, Yancey, and Aslyn was in my computer, and I couldn't recall leaving it there. My plants looked fabulous and healthy; even my Venus flytrap smuggled in from Topsail Island was thriving. My newspapers were neatly folded and stacked on my desk.

To restore my spirit, I took a short hike on a branch of the Baker Field Park Trail and touched the barks of several Madronas, even peeled off a few pieces to put near my computer. When I returned, I made a dozen Nanaimo bars and took them to the office, my first of several thank you gifts for Melanie.

She told me, "I just accepted a job offer in Virginia, and today is my last day in Point Roberts."

She snuggled up to me near the reception desk and whispered, "I have to be in Richmond day after tomorrow, the 18th."

She put my hand on her shapely ass, "So, please give me a happy send off, maybe more, before I go. I'm sure I can lift your spirits."

Caden's Comments

OMG! These last entries prove Jamie right. Dr. Ahh lied to and manipulated them while pretending to be Ben's greedy mirror image. All of them fell for it. Only Jamie saw the Cabal's danger to them. Ben's take on Yancey during their last interview is unnerving and shows he was beginning to understand the Cabal. I'd love to tattoo Yancey's forehead as Ben imagined. It's hard to believe someone as smart as Ben didn't resist the Cabal until both his new friends died.

I'll send these entries to Aslyn and M.J. to get their take on them. I'll ask them for a quick turnaround. I think I'm one step closer to finding out who killed Ben and why.

Crap! Both Jamie and Jackson are dead! I wish the three of them had never met.

CADEN'S QUEST ENDS

(JANUARY 1, 2021 TO JANUARY 12, 2021)

CHAPTER 11:
ASLYN'S PERCEPTIONS
(JANUARY 1, 2021)

Caden opens his Zoom invite at 6:00 pm and sees Aslyn on the screen. "Happy New Year, Doc! Hope you had a good New Year's Eve like Tyrone and I did."

Tyrone stands behind Aslyn, tipping Caden and her with two glasses of champagne, which he chugs down with amazing speed, then belches, a sound rivaling an echo from a thunder mug.

Caden gushes, "It's so good to see you two. What's up?"

"You were right to send me your notes and Ben's journal entries. I'm Zooming you now because I'll probably go into labor this week. As you can see, Tyrone's a nervous wreck!"

She speaks faster than usual, excited about her findings. He can't even get a word in.

"Occam is powerful, but he works only if you see patterns before you. Like you said, 'Shave away everything that doesn't fit an obvious pattern.' I'm going to sound like Jackson and Jamie, so bear with me."

Tyrone brings her a Diet Pepsi, gives a thumbs up to Caden, and moves out of the frame.

"Dr. Humphrey, thanks to Jamie, really earned his new name, Ass Hole Humphrey. Dr. Ahh has power. He selects and reassigns wealthy interns, visits graveyards in other cities, and seems wealthy.

"Humphrey never remarried and has a daughter whose mother died giving birth to her. She's now 27 years old, graduated from Duke, married a lawyer. Her avatar appeared on the CPA's Facebook page until 2018, when she temporarily moved to the Pacific Northwest to interface with Salish Sea psychics. Her husband, Yancey Jenkins, stayed here in Richmond. Her name is Melanie, and she often goes by M.J."

Caden opens his mouth wide and breathes in slowly. He whispers, "Dammit! She manipulated me and Ben, and we didn't catch on."

Aslyn goes on, "Dr. Ahh secretly knows everyone. We need to find out if he really travelled to Southern cemeteries or elsewhere and see if his trips coincide with Council meetings. He's a member of the Council of 5, really the Cabal of 6. He's a manipulator and uses his daughter M.J./Melanie and his son-in-law Yancey to move their agenda. I'll bet your scrawny white ass Humphrey is one of the brains behind the Cabal."

Squirming, he hardly hears Aslyn as he wonders if the small scar on M.J.'s lovely ass was from having sex with Ben on the beach at the Point. She probably cut her ass on a small shell in a moment of passion. On a Salt Lake walk Ben once confessed he was SOB #6, a member of the "Sex on Beach" Society at the Naval Air Station in Norfolk. Crap, crap…now maybe he's SOB #7.

Aslyn stops, "Are you O.K., Doc? You look like you're going to throw up!"

He shakes his head "No, I'm just thinking."

"You can't fix stupid" echoes in his mind. The thought of him and Ben sleeping with the same lover makes it hard for him to swallow. M.J. moved to Seattle the morning after their last F2F. He was in the shower when she disappeared, and she took his favorite souvenir robe with her. "How the hell did I miss this pattern?"

Aslyn's voice sounds far away, "Yancey Jenkins is Dr. Ahh's relative and a hard core MAGAite. In fact, Yancey invented this new version of MAGA. A list of cases he has worked on points out his connection to the VDP. He's sued the Southern Poverty Law Center, the ACLU, and the Bernie Sanders campaign numerous times. He's now honing in on AOC. He's currently trying to override rulings that allow the removal of Southern monuments from public spaces. He's challenged the definition of voter suppression and voter fraud in several Virginia courts, and has spent the past few years redefining disability accommodations.

"He advocates greater use of psychics in U.S. intelligence, probably to gain military industrial support from Department of Defense independent contractors, but that's just my veteran interpretation. The Cabal, based on Yancey's lawsuits, is secretly introducing the Voting Dead Act as a new kind of gerrymandering to ensure their wealth."

Back on track, Caden nods and bites the tip of his right thumb.

She continues, "M.J./Melanie is their family member who thinks on the spot and uses her looks to manipulate you and Ben, which doesn't surprise me, to make sure the Cabal's wishes are met."

Aslyn pauses to catch her breath, takes a sip of her Diet Pepsi, "M.J.'s a secret informer, who read your notes to me as a surveillance strategy to remove threats to the VDP. I can see why you call Ben 'BCB.' His actions show he really is 'Butt Chaser Ben.'"

Caden sputters, "No, no, 'BCB' means 'Buck Chaser Ben,' a reference to his focus on money!"

"Crap, Doc, I'm so sorry. I just misheard. Tyrone will be so disappointed. Only you and Ben know what else she's done to keep you OBs distracted and off guard. I really don't want to know those details, but Tyrone thinks it'd be dope if you sent him your notes and photos, if you have any.

"It gets creepier. Dr. Ahh might have been responsible for both Jamie and Jackson's deaths. He used Jamie's death as a warning to Jackson. But naïve, optimistic Jackson didn't see the connection between his tenure file, proposal, blog, and Jamie's death. Who else but Humphrey and Ben knew about Jackson's tenure file? He was so enamored with his asshole mentor that it wouldn't surprise me if he blamed Ben for Jamie's death.

"Doc, you missed the warning, too. And as usual, the Black man died first. Humphrey was a major player in Ben's death, too. It's not coincidental Ben died in the Pacific Northwest and worked with someone named Melanie. By the way, did you ever check the demographics of Point Roberts because it's an unbelievably small white town? The Cabal probably moved Melanie there to keep an eye on Ben."

Caden nods, "Those turd merchants. I get it now. We're living in the perfect time for the Cabal to achieve its goals. Covid puts emotions before critical thinking. Some thinking people see the pandemic as a time to critique unbridled capitalism, a broken system, that promotes hunger, homelessness, lack of medical health coverage, unemployment, education debt, and human needs in general."

Aslyn leans into the computer camera and interrupts, "Others see the shutdown and medical mandates—masks, social distancing, vaccinations—as personal attacks on their freedoms and liberties. Hell, some people yearn for their romantic version of the Lost Cause. Sounds like a plot for a contemporary dystopian horror film.

"These perspectives co-exist. Somewhere in all this we forget our shared humanity as Jackson, Dr. King, Gandhi, and Jesus pointed out. Politicians sometimes forget they represent people, not just themselves."

She sips her soft drink and continues, "We're ignoring the next generation, the youth, the agents of future change, who have to watch, absorb, and live with whatever our takeaways will be. A twenty-year-old has spent 10% of their life in pandemic bunker mode and all their life watching friends and family members fight in wars since 9/11. Like the high school students sang in the zombie musical *Anna and the Apocalypse,* 'There's no such thing as a Hollywood ending!' But their day is coming, just as ours did."

Caden agrees, "The under 30 demographic is making sure they're not 'out of sight and out of mind.' Thanks to their actions, there's hope on the horizon!"

"Damn, we sound like we're lecturing each other! Doc, be careful. You told me you're submitting a paper to the *Disability Studies Quarterly.* I know your research aligns with the journal's mission to promote 'the full and equal participation of persons with disabilities in society.' Your paper might sound the alarm for readers when they see this new twist on the ADAA and its threat to living people with disabilities. Beware of the Cabal's response to your article if *DSQ* publishes it. I think Ben, Jackson, and Jamie's deaths are a warning to you.

"Gotta go...only 49 seconds left on this session. Next time you see me, I'll be holding your niece!" As Aslyn ends the Zoom, Caden hears Tyrone shout, "Y'all stay cool, Uncle Caden!"

CHAPTER 12:
GUGU IS BORN!
(JANUARY 5, 2021)

Hey, Doc, or should I say Uncle Caden?

Just a quick update. Aslyn's in the hospital with our beautiful daughter, Gugu Caden Jones-Williams. Both of them are well and asleep. You're going to love holding our little one. I love the way she wraps her tiny fingers around my little finger. I'm going home to prepare a homecoming for all of you tomorrow!

As planned, we'll move out at the end of the month. You'll like the new place Aslyn found for us in the Fan District, just six blocks from your office. We're all looking forward to seeing you. I'll pick you up at the airport tomorrow evening. Even with a mask on, my smile will be lighting up the baggage area, so you won't have any problem finding me.

Daddy Tyrone

CHAPTER 13:
ANOTHER SLAP IN THE FACE
(JANUARY 6, 2021)

On January 6, Caden sits at a teriyaki bar in Sea-Tac, sips a local IPA, watches masked passengers run to gates, and catches up on text messages while waiting for his flight to Richmond. He looks forward to hearing more about Aslyn and Gugu. He imagines how incredible his house looks because Tyrone's sense of style outstrips everyone he's ever known.

Tyrone raises feng shui to a new level. Caden smiles every time he thinks of him and Aslyn as a couple. He still has a hard time seeing a Marine sniper with a Silver Star as an interior designer, an idea Aslyn calls "your limited stereotypical vision." He sees flowers, candy, smells homemade muffins sitting on his dining room table, and hears Black Violins softly filling the air.

His *Richmond Times Dispatch* app says he has 36 new alerts, probably all focused on the crowds gathering at the Capitol in D.C. today protesting the "stolen" election, which plays on all the screens in the airport. He's so fixated on Aslyn and Tyrone he's ignored most things in the past week.

He's having difficulty seeing a break-in of the Capitol as anything but domestic terrorism, not just vandalism. He wonders if the Cabal had anything to do with it. Even some journalists and politicians describe the attacks as overreactions of "excited tourists." How are anarchy, insurrection, murder, breaking in, and general brawling "tourism"? What the hell are these reporters and politicians drinking or smoking?

Caden thinks, "In the next few months, we'll probably see a new genre of blame blossoming on social media, new ways of interpreting and ignoring criminal acts. I yearn for the old days. Hell, I even miss the barrage of daily Tweets from the Twitter King, who simply misread 'meme' as 'me, me.'"

An old memory flits across Caden's mind like a summer lightning bug at dusk. He remembers the July 4th in Jacksonville when a policeman saw him removing little foot-high U.S. flags from his Confederate great, great uncles' raised graves in a parking lot behind abandoned stores on Old Bridge Street.

"Boy, you know what you're doing is breaking the law? Put those damn flags back, or you'll sleep in jail this weekend until you get arraigned for vandalism or grave desecration, but in all likelihood, domestic terrorism."

"No sir, I'm celebrating July 4th, an American holiday. Just showing the difference between U.S. veterans and U.S. enemies. Besides, I'm not throwing the flags away. I put them in the corner of the plot. I don't think I'm a vandal or a terrorist. I like to think what I'm doing is a private family matter."

Three days later the judge slapped him on the wrist, "Case dismissed! In the future keep private family problems out of sight." He then charged him court costs.

Caden wishes he had thought about Occam then. He still has a hard time seeing how the cop thought the incident was domestic terrorism, but now realizes the cop was one of many people who feel the same way. You see what you want to see or are programmed to see, even if the facts are shouting your name, staring at you, and showing you something else! It's like a falling apple.

When he told Aslyn this story last year, she said, "Doc, $150 court cost is nothing. If you were Black, you'd still be on one of the city jail's cleaning crews or more likely teaching from your wheelchair because you got shot for removing U.S. flags from Confederate graves. You should be thankful you weren't removing Confederate flags from those graves!"

He thumb scrolls through the articles on his cell, and stops at *"Burglar Killed at James River's Edge Estates."* Thank God, Tyrone and Asyln were at the Henrico Hospital. He never expected a shooting in his area. The shouts and boos from the crowd of passengers standing in front of the large screen near his gate distract him. He stares as the mob assaults the Capitol and wonders if he's watching a social media nightmare sponsored by the Cabal.

Shaken and disgusted, Caden turns back to the *Times Dispatch* article and sees another nightmare:

"Tyrone Martin Jones was killed last night as he broke into a new townhome in James River's Edge Estates. At 9:30 pm, Jones, carrying a large bouquet of roses and pretending to be a delivery person for a florist, was shot while searching for a brick to break through the backdoor window. A neighbor who had just moved in called the estate's surveillance team, who confronted Jones and shot him six times as he flipped over another brick, while shouting, 'I'm searching for our key! My wife, my baby, and I live here!' The Henrico County Sheriff's Department is investigating the incident."

"Tyrone!" He bumps his forehead up and down on the counter and murmurs, "Oh my God...oh my God...oh my God." People sitting at the bar move away. He can't help himself.

Caden has no family now except Gugu and Aslyn, who must be in deep shock. When he gets to Richmond, he'll go straight to

Henrico Hospital, help her pack, and take her and Gugu home. He wants to hold them both and apologize for asking her and Tyrone to stay at his house. He wants to time travel and exchange places with Tyrone.

He stares across the restaurant at the flight screen by the seating area and realizes he needs to call Aslyn now to support her and let her talk about Tyrone and Gugu, who's now fatherless. Shaking his head, he turns on his swivel chair, runs to the men's room, and throws up inside the doorway, realizing that every year when Gugu celebrates her birthday, she'll remember it's also the anniversary of her father's murder.

CHAPTER 14:
HOME FROM THE HOSPITAL
(JANUARY 7, 2021)

Caden arrives after midnight and the next morning picks up Gugu and Aslyn at Henrico Hospital. She's in silent shock, trying not to put her burden on Gugu. When they get home, she goes upstairs and puts Gugu in the baby crib Tyrone designed. She'd never seen it until now, and she smiles at Tyrone's view of their family painted on the crib. Muted colors and perfectly spaced drawings of flowers, sea shells, baby bears, kittens, and puppies create a feng shui tribute to Gugu, who smiles and twitches when Asyln lays her in it.

Later that morning, sniffing and folding Tyrone's clothes, she tells Caden, "I'm so glad you came back early. We're going to need you for a few weeks until we move into our new home and rethink our lives without him."

Then, for the first time, he sees her cry. She fights back tears and screams, "My Tyrone! My Tyrone!" She upsets Gugu, who now screams. He watches them, cheek to cheek crying, and goes downstairs, having never been so sad. They're his only family now.

CHAPTER 15:
NO ONE'S HOME
(JANUARY 8, 2021)

Tonight, he'll convince Aslyn she and Gugu should stay in his house for a few months until her life feels more normal. He'll help her slowly move into her Fan home. His class on "The Role of Disability in Contemporary Horror Films" starts on January 25, so he needs to spend more time at his office and VCU's library. As soon as he completes his syllabus and his reading list, they'll discuss her role, if she wants one, in his overenrolled virtual class.

As Caden leaves his townhouse that morning, Aslyn mutters, "Thanks for offering to house me and Gugu, but I don't think I can live here anymore. This house is where Tyrone suffered and took his last breath." She, and then Gugu, cry. He nods remembering his Mom's words, "Don't bring horror home."

He hugs them, "I'll always be your backup, and I'll help you move into your new home in the Fan. This evening, I'll bring home your favorite pizza and a pint of spumoni." She points out spumoni was Tyrone's favorite, not hers, then sobs again.

Sitting outside the library, he texts her at 3:00 and gets no response. She's probably taking boxes to her Fan house and left her cell at his townhouse. He really wants to tell her about his ideas for his new paper on Catholicism and Vampirism, but knows now is not the time.

For years he's wondered about Eucharist and drinking wine as a symbol of blood. Does drinking blood have two meanings? The first, representing Christ, the second Satan? What if a priest pours blood instead of wine into the golden chalice during Communion? Is the worshipper taking communion that day changed forever? Is this the first step towards vampirism, the eternal body, not the eternal soul?

Caden recalls Alan Ryan's "Following the Way," a vampire story about priests who blur the body/spirit binary. He knows he and Aslyn could put together a fascinating horror film course with films questioning spirituality. He knows she'll probably start with *The Exorcist*, although possession is not what he has in mind. He'll put the course on the back burner until next year. As he drives home, he smiles thinking about *Jesus Christ Vampire Hunter*, the quirky Canadian film, where Jesus returns as a martial arts expert to promote love and protect young women from vampires threatening Ottawa's lesbian community.

When he can no longer distract himself with horror films, he realizes he has to confront his new reality. He gets home at 6:00 and sees Aslyn's car is in the garage. She and Gugu aren't in the house. In the living room most of her and Tyrone's belongings are packed, ready for the move. Lying on one box from the clothes rack is Tyrone's dress blues. He calls her cell, and gets no answer, so he leaves a voice mail. He also texts her a message. She doesn't come home that night, and he freaks out. Worrying about her and Gugu, he stays dressed and keeps his phone beside his pillow all night.

CHAPTER 16:
CADEN'S SEARCH
(JANUARY 9, 2021)

By noon, he and Aslyn haven't been in contact for nearly 24 hours. He's almost crazy thinking about her and Gugu's safety. What could have happened to them? Why have they gone? Are they safe? Why have we lost touch?

He drops by her new house in the Fan District, and through the living room window sees Gugu's crib beside several boxes of clothes and two brass reading lamps. Lying on top of a box is a hooded black robe, like the one you imagine Death wearing in horror films. Tyrone was a local hero in the Richmond theater community for this robe. He designed it for Virginia University's production of Shakespeare's *Henry IV, Part 2*. Worn by the character Rumor in the Prologue, his robe set the pace and tone, hitting the audience hard.

Rather than covering the robe with tongues, Tyrone sewed on social media logos—FB, Twitter, TikTok, Instagram, LinkedIn, and even QAnon—but still kept a few tongues on it. His colorful hem border boasted red and yellow flames. When the actor playing Rumor answered his cell phone near the edge of the stage, he picked sugar crumbs off his robe and muttered:

"Upon my tongues continual slanders ride...
The posts come tiring on,
And not a man of them brings other news
Than they have learnt of me. From
Rumour's tongues
They bring smooth comforts false, worse
than true wrongs."

Caden smiled because that event was the first the three of them ever attended together. Later, eating comfort food snacks at the Bamboo Cafe, Tyrone and Aslyn asked him if he'd consider being the godfather of their future children. Caden can hardly swallow as he returns to his car thinking about Tyrone.

As soon as he arrives home and realizes Aslyn is still absent, he calls the police to explain her and Gugu's disappearance. A raspy voiced officer drawls, "Don't y'all worry. Delivering a baby and losing its father on the same day is devastating. She probably just needs more alone time."

The officer continues, "We can begin our legal search for them late tomorrow afternoon."

Caden hangs up, hurls his cell at his sofa, and kicks his mom's handmade decorated floor pillow across the room. After thirty minutes of silence, he opens a Diet Dr. Pepper, and finishes last night's pizza and spumoni. An hour later, he knocks on neighbors' doors, avoiding the one who called the security team on Tyrone. No one saw anything unusual; most were at work anyway. An older silver-haired dog walker passing by tells him, "I saw a Black woman with a baby get into a black van with two well-dressed white men just after lunch yesterday." As she picked up dog poop, she mumbled, "Her baby wasn't even wearing a mask!"

Back home, he pours himself a glass of wine and sits at his kitchen table. He can barely focus. He pulls out Aslyn's notes on

Humphrey, Jenkins, and M.J. to see if anything jumps out. At the end of his observations is her interpretation of the notes and her perspective. He wishes he had read her notes more closely earlier.

His muffled phone vibrates. He sees a voice note from M.J., and he ignores it. A few minutes later she texts him:

"Darlin' Dr. Caden is Aslyn all right?

I haven't heard from her in nine days since she sent me her comments on my research about Ben Dunn, Jamie Nealy, and Jackson Canaday. She was polite, but I think she virtually bitch slapped me—pardon my language—and angered Dr. Humphrey and Yancey Jenkins when I shared her notes with them.

Call me soon. UW has started and I need to pay my rent in Seattle. I'm moving into my apartment next week, so you can send me money through PayPal.

Thanks for all you've done for me. I hope my work has helped you, too.

Love,
M.J."

Dammit! Her message makes no sense. He sips wine and asks, "Why is she telling me she shared Asyln's notes with Humphrey and Yancey?" He swirls his glass, then gulps the rest of the wine, "Shit, I get it: M.J.'s giving me the finger with this text." He imagines her shaking her head and smiling as she pushed the send button.

No wonder Asyln and Gugu have disappeared. You don't have to be an Occam fan to see they were next. He swallows hard, knowing he is now the only player left.

CHAPTER 17:
THE LAST CODED LETTER
(JANUARY 11, 2021)

The weekend creeps by and Caden hasn't heard a word from Aslyn or a gurgle from Gugu. The police department calls and leaves a message on his office phone, "We've begun a search for Ms. Williams and her infant."

When he returns home from his office, Caden notices an envelope someone slipped under his door. Since he lives in a gated community, it's probably a party invitation from a neighbor. Inside is this coded message, a short list of odd words: "WITSEC, poutine, eh, Nanaimo, Gugu."

On the reverse side is: *^ $ 2*.

"Who delivered this note, and why does it end with Ben's signature code? He's dead for crap's sake, nearly a year and a half now! He's an effing discarnate! I don't get it. What is WITSEC? What does it have to do with me?"

Google tells him WITSEC is an acronym for the Federal Witness Security Program.

His vision swirls. Too much is happening—Ben, Jamie, Jackson, and now Tyrone are dead. Aslyn and Gugu have disappeared, for gods' sake, maybe dead. He wants to be alone, scream, and drink.

It's two weeks before class begins, and all he thinks about is Aslyn and his baby niece. "How can I teach a horror film class? My life's a horror! What the hell did I do to deserve this? It's some kind of cosmic joke—comeuppance for all the stupid things I've done in life. Dammit, Ben, if you just stayed in Seattle none of this crap would have happened. We had amazing plans for your 50th birthday party at the U. of U. All 12 of us were planning to show up in Salt Lake City and treat you to a vegan foodfest."

It occurs to Caden he's playing the Blame Game. He apologizes to Ben and the cosmos.

Jackson, Jamie, and Aslyn would all calm him down and say, "Think like Occam…TLO…TLO!" He moves all the furniture out of the dining room and on the polished wooden floor lays in columns copies of all Ben's journal entries, his own notes, Yancey's responses to his questions, M.J.'s research info, and Aslyn's notes. He pours a huge glass of Merlot, stares at the notes, and whispers, "Think like Occam. Think like Occam. TLO…Be the Razor."

He lists everything in the notes occurring more than twice to see if he'd missed some obvious patterns. Getting a buzz on from the wine, he keeps whispering, "Think like Occam. What is obvious, what is obvious! TLO!"

Grouping recurring items, he sees ominous patterns emerge:

1) Manipulating the moment—fingering rings to signal Cabal members at Martha's Vineyard, the husband signaling his wife at the pizza place on Topsail, and M.J. and the geezers signaling each other at Cafe Kaffeine

2) Deaths of friends/partners as warnings to Ben, Jackson, Aslyn, and him, if he read M.J.'s last text correctly

3) Systemic racism—don't even need Occam for this one: deaths of innocent Black men first, Jamie and Tyrone, and God knows, maybe even Aslyn and Gugu. VDP's emphasis on white dead men who fear Black voters, ignore Black deaths, and privilege white deaths

4) Ben's and his own naive sexist patriarchal views of beautiful women diverted them from seeing what was right before them, i.e., Melanie's access to his computer, odd details from M.J.'s audition (knowing Ben and he used written codes)

5) Signs of Cabal wealth—the Vineyard Haven location and private helicopters, chauffeured gull-wing Mercedes, Humphrey's boat, and Ben's salary

6) Privileged white male participants—Humphrey, Ben, Jackson, and Yancey (and oddly even himself)

7) The deceptive and hidden role of family: i.e., Humphrey, Yancey, and M.J./Melanie, Yancey knowing Jamie's name

8) "The Spy"—M.J./Melanie who informs her father's Cabal of imminent security breaches like sending Dr. Ahh Aslyn's notes and Jackson's tenure file.

It's obvious: the Cabal secretly manipulates its employees and kills anyone questioning its methods or derailing its project. They make their employees' deaths look like random accidents. Each death was a warning signal to the rest of them to remain quiet, but none of them saw it. Jamie's death didn't stop Jackson from misapplying Occam; nor did Jackson's death occur to Ben as a warning. Maybe Tyrone's death allowed Aslyn to see the obvious.

It took four deaths and Aslyn and Gugu's disappearance for him to see the pattern. If he heard tense music, it'd be the soundtrack from John Carpenter's *Halloween* movies.

Exhausted, he goes upstairs to sleep. He wants a clearer head as he thinks through this clusterfuck. More questions pop up, and just before dawn, he has his clarifying moment! In bed, he reads the coded note again; this time between the lines, shaving off theories, and focusing on the obvious. He looks for patterns. Then it hits him. He understands what the note's telling him and urging him to do: "WITSEC, poutine, eh, Nanaimo, Gugu." As stereotyped as "eh" is, it works for him.

CHAPTER 18:
"AN OCCAM MOMENT"
(JANUARY 12, 2021)

He wakes up with a new purpose in mind. Over the next three hours, he packs a bag with warm clothes, shoves six N95 masks into his REI commuter pack, showers, and gets his passport ready. He closes all the blinds, and at noon he drives to the nearest Capitol One Bank. He withdraws $20,000 in $100 bills from his savings account, puts them into two bundles, secures them with big rubber bands, and crams them into his pack. Watching him, the young assistant manager's eyes dance above her mask.

On the way home, he picks up several days of hiking snacks and dried foods at the Co-op. Around 3:00, he pulls into the fourth floor of VCU's biggest parking deck and slips into a faculty space. He grabs his food, leaves his car, and texts Uber, "Pick me up at 3:30. I'll be at Monroe Park on Franklin Street, sitting on a bench at the middle entrance. I'm wearing a lighted solar system mask."

After the Uber picks him up, they cross the James River, and several miles later enter James River's Edge Estates. He directs his masked driver, "Go slowly through my neighborhood. I'll tell you where to drop me off."

Everyone is at work; no one is even walking a dog. Kids are on their way home from school. The streets are almost deserted. She drops him off two blocks from his front door and delivers the food, setting the bag under the leafless azalea beside his garage door, as told. It's 4:15 p.m. when he gets home. The street lights turn on as he opens the garage door. He walks across the cement floor and enters his home through the inside kitchen door.

He doesn't turn on house lights or open the blinds. He surrounds himself with snacks, a six-pack of sugar-free vitamin water, and two bottles of Merlot. He puts his gear at the bottom of the stairs and waits for a phone call telling him a black SUV or another vehicle is on its way to pick him up.

Ben's coded note screams at him and gives him hope. It took a while, but he gets it. Even though he doesn't know who slipped the note under his door, he sees a pattern no one else could have. He's sure he'll see Ben, Aslyn, and Gugu soon. Maybe they can be a family somewhere, and he can watch Gugu grow up. He sees them sitting at an outdoor table on a cold beach or in the foothills of a Canadian mountain range, and hears Gugu call, "Uncle Caden" as she brings him one of Ben's vegan Nanaimo bars.

He glances at the note and hopes he's reading Occam right this time and not just woolgathering. He pushes his gear closer to his front door and plops down on the bottom stairstep for a quick exit. He goes through his Nestor routine, inhales deeply and exhales, and holds his little fingers to his thumbs. He opens a bottle of Merlot, raises his glass, "To you, Ben, my Orphan Brother," as someone softly knocks on his front door and turns the doorknob.

BACKGROUND READINGS AND WEBSITES

This list of books, articles, and websites provides general background information and insights into characters' ideologies, discussions, and actions. During the pandemic, these sources helped shape *The Voting Dead Project*.

General Background

Bregman, Rutger. *Humankind: A Hopeful History*. Back Bay Books, Little, Brown & Company. New York. 2020.

Donnella, Leah. "All Mixed Up: What Do We Call People Of Multiple Backgrounds?" Code Switch: Word Watch, *NPR*. August 25, 2016 (7:00 AM ET).

Dresser, Norine. *American Vampire, Fans, Victims, Practitioners*. Vintage Books (Division of Random House), New York, 1990.

Duignan, Brian, "Dunning-Kruger Effect." *Britannica*. Visited 1/30/2023. https://www.britannica.com/science/Dunning-Kruger-effect

Hamad, Ruby. *White Tears/Brown Scars: How White Feminism Betrays Women of Color*. Catapult, New York, 2020.

Hartmann, Thom. *The Hidden History of the War on Voting: Who Stole Your Vote and How to Get It Back*. Berrett-Koehler Publishers, Oakland, CA, 2020.

Kendi, Ibram X. *How to Be an Antiracist*. One Word, New York, 2019.

Pitstick, Mark. "SoulPhone Project Updates." The SoulPhone Foundation. Visited 1/31/2023. https://www.thesoulphonefoundation.org/soulphone-update/

Shapiro, James. *Shakespeare in a Divided America: What His Plays Tell Us About Our Past and Future*. Penguin, New York, 2020.

The 1619 Project: A New Origin Story. Edited by Hannah-Jones, Nikole, Caitlin Roper, Ilena Silverman, and Jake Silverstein. One World, New York, 2021.

The Decision Lab. "Why can we not perceive our own abilities? (The Dunning–Kruger Effect Explained)." Visited 2/5/2023. https://thedecisionlab.com/biases/dunning-kruger-effect

"The DOPS Mission-Scientific Study of Extraordinary Experiences."
Division of Perceptual Studies, University of Virginia. Visited 1/31/2023.
https://med.virginia.edu/perceptual-studies/

"The National Voter Registration Act Of 1993 (NVRA)." The United States
Department of Justice. Visited 1/25/2023. https://www.justice.gov/crt/
national-voter-registration-act-1993-nvra

"Travel and Tourism." International Trade Administration. https://www.trade.gov/
travel-tourism-industry. Visited January 22, 2023.

Civil War Cemeteries & Memorials

"Civil War Era National Cemeteries: Honoring Those Who Served." National Park
Service, U. S. Department of the Interior. Visited 12/22/2022. https://www.nps.
gov/nr/travel/national_cemeteries/list_of_sites.html

"Confederate Memorial: Section 16." Arlington National Cemetery. Visited
12/22/2022. https://www.arlingtoncemetery.mil/Explore/Monuments-and-
Memorials/Confederate-Memorial

"Hollywood Cemetery." Hollywood Cemetery Company, Richmond, VA.
Visited 12/22/2022. https://www.hollywoodcemetery.org/

"In the Spirit of Freedom." African American Civil War Memorial. Visited
12/22/2022. https://www.nps.gov/afam/index.htm

"Section 27." Arlington National Cemetery. Visited 11/30/2022. https://www.
arlingtoncemetery.mil/Explore/History-of-Arlington-National-Cemetery/
Section-27

"Wilmington National Cemetery, Wilmington, North Carolina." National Park
Service. Department of the Interior. Visited 12/22/2022. https://www.nps.
gov/nr/travel/national_cemeteries/North_Carolina/Wilmington_National_
Cemetery.html

Disability Issues

Baynton, Douglas Dr. "Education Essay: 'Language Matters: Handicapping An
Affliction.'" Disability History Museum. Also appears as "Beyond Affliction,"
Interview, *National Public Radio*, 1998. (Visited 12/22/2022). https://www.
disabilitymuseum.org/dhm/edu/essay.html?id=30

Davis, Leonard J. *Bending Over Backwards: Disability, Dismodernism, and Other
Difficult Positions.* New York University Press, 2002.

Francis, Leslie and PhD, JD and Anita Silvers, PhD. *"Perspectives on the Meaning of Disability.'" AMA Journal of Ethics*, October, 2016. Visited 12/22/2022. https://journalofethics.ama-assn.org/article/perspectives-meaning-disability/2016-10

Stiker, Heni-Jacques. Trans. William Sayers. *A History of Disability*. University of Michigan Press, Ann Arbor, 2009.

"The Americans with Disabilities Act (ADA) protects people with disabilities from discrimination." U.S. Department of Justice: Civil, Rights Division. Visited 12/22/2022. https://www.ada.gov/

"The Americans with Disabilities Act Amendments Act of 2008." U.S. Equal Employment Opportunity Commission. Visited 12/22/2022. https://www. eeoc.gov/statutes/americans-disabilities-act-amendments-act-2008

Vaughan, C. Edwin. "Are We Handicapped, Disabled, or Something Else?" *Braille Monitor*. Visited 12/22/2022. https://nfb.org/sites/default/files/images/nfb/publications/bm/bm19/bm1901/bm190111.htm

Fiction

Buckley, Christopher. *Boomsday*. Twelve Hachette Book Group, 2007.

Carr, A.A. *Eye Killers*. American Indian Literature and Critical Studies Series. University of Oklahoma Press, Norman, OK, 1996.

Doctorow, E. L. *The March*. Random House, New York, 2005.

Ford, Clyde W. *Red Herring*. Mystic Voyager Books. mysticvoyagerbooks.com. 2005.
—*Precious Cargo*. Vanguard Press, New York, NY, 2008.
—*Whiskey Gulf*. Vanguard Press, New York, NY, 2009.

Meyer, Stephenie. *Twilight* (Book 1 of the *Twilight Saga Series*). Little, Brown Books for Young Readers, Boston, MA, 2005.

Ryan, Alan, editor. *The Penguin Book of Vampire Stories: Two Centuries of Great Stories with a Bite*. Penguin Books, London, England, 1988. ("Following the Way," pp. 562-573).

Saunders, George. *Lincoln in the Bardo*. Random House, New York, NY, 2017.

Stoker, Bram. *Dracula. (Dover Thrift Editions: Classic Novels)*. Mineola, New York, 2000.

Horror Film History

Coleman, Robin R. Means. *Horror Noire: Blacks in American Horror Films from the 1890s to Present* [Foreword by S. Torriano Berry]. Routledge, New York, NY, 2011.

Marine Corps

Simmons, Edwin Howard. *The United States Marines: A History.* 4th Edition. Naval Institute Press, Annapolis, MD, 2003.

The Montford Point Marine Memorial. City of Jacksonville, North Carolina. Visited 12/22/2022. https://visitjacksonvillenc.com/165/Montford-Point-Marine-Memorial

"The Montford Point Marine Memorial." The National Montford Point Marine Association, Inc. Visited 12/22/2022. https://montfordpointmarines.org/page-18093

N.C. and VA. Resources

Dance, Daryl Cumber. *Long Gone: the Mecklenburg Six and the Theme of Escape in Black Folklore.* The University of Tennessee Press, Knoxville. TN, 1987.

Gordon, Lesley J. "George E. Pickett (1825-1875)." *Encyclopedia Virginia* (A Program of the Virginia Humanities), 2020. Visited: 1/31/2023. https://encyclopediavirginia.org/entries/pickett-george-e-1825-1875/

Harter, Eugene C. *The Lost Colony of the Confederacy.* Texas A&M University Press, College Station, TX, 2003.

Hughey, Patricia M. *Onslow County (Images of America).* Arcadia Publishing, Charleston, S.C. 2016.

Jennet, Norman Ethre. "The Vampire that Hovers Over North Carolina," *Textbook.* Visited December 22, 2022. http://historymaking.org/textbook/items/show/264.

Tise, Larry E. and Jefferey J. Crowe, eds. *New Voyages to Carolina: Reinterpreting North Carolina History.* University of North Carolina Press, Chapel Hill, 2017.